What Did You Do
BEFORE DYING?

A Marge Christensen Mystery

What Did You Do
BEFORE DYING?

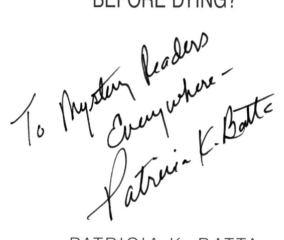

*To Mystery Readers
Everywhere –
Patricia K. Batta*

PATRICIA K. BATTA

LILLIMAR PUBLISHING
Traverse City, Michigan

Lillimar Publishing
Traverse City, Mich.

Cataloging-in-Publication Data

Batta, Patricia K.

What did you do before dying? : a Marge Christensen mystery / Patricia K.
Batta — Traverse City, Mich. : Lillimar Publishing, c2008.

p. ; cm.

ISBN: 978-0-9797883-0-7

1. Christensen, Marge (Fictitious character)—Fiction.
2. Widows—Fiction. 3. Suicide—Fiction. 4. Bellevue (Wash.)—Fiction.
5. Mystery fiction. I. Title.

PS3602.A898 W43 2008   2007932528
813.54—dc22   0712

Printed in the United States of America
10 9 8 7 6 5 4 3 2 1

BOOK DESIGN BY TO THE POINT SOLUTIONS
www.tothepointsolutions.com

This is a work of fiction. Names, characters, places, and incidents either are the
product of the author's imagination or are used fictitiously, and any resemblance
to actual persons, living or dead, businesses, companies, events, or locales is
entirely coincidental.

In memory of my husband, Narinder K. Batta,
who gave me the confidence and time
to fulfill my dream.

ACKNOWLEDGMENTS

I OWE TOO MUCH thanks for help and encouragement to too many people to list them here. However, I would like to give special thanks to Mary Jo Zazueta, editor and self-publishing guide, who helped me and led me through the process with tact and humor.

What Did You Do
BEFORE DYING?

CHAPTER 1

MARGE TRIED TO stop the rerun. She turned her back on the soft morning sunlight slanting through the bedroom window and burrowed into a tangle of blankets and sheets, seeking a return to warmth and oblivion.

Moments later, she sighed, unable to ban the nightmare that plagued her continuously: waking at two in the morning to find the other side of the bed empty. Her feet on the stairs. Opening the garage door. The odor. Gene, in the car, slumped over. The scream. *Her* scream.

There was only one way to stop reliving it. She swung her feet out of bed to meet the day.

The bathroom mirror reflected a green-eyed stranger with a pale freckled face. She brushed her teeth, ran her fingers through a jumbled mass of untamed auburn curls, and shrugged. Who was there now to care? Slipping into the comfort of an old rumpled robe, she slid her feet into a pair of worn mules and padded down the stairs.

She started the coffeemaker and switched on the radio. She tuned it to a station that played the music she had pretended not to enjoy when the children were teenagers. The volume, dialed up to defeat the silence, reverberated throughout the house. The doorbell rang.

"Good morning."

Marge swallowed to suppress the groan that rose in her throat at the sound of Caroline's clipped voice. Opening the door wider revealed narrowed icy-blue eyes that seemed to measure her from head to foot.

"I hope I didn't wake you. Robert wanted me to look in on you before going to work." She glanced over Marge's shoulder. "Is someone here? What is that . . . that noise?"

Caroline's tailored gray suit and elegant white blouse made Marge painfully aware of how she must look to her daughter-in-law. Time passed slowly while she tried to find her voice.

"No, no one's here. Just me clearing out the cobwebs," she finally managed. "As it happens, I am up this morning. Would you like a cup of coffee?"

"Oh, no. I have to get to work."

"If time is a problem, I should think the telephone would have been a more efficient means of checking up on me." Marge wanted to bite her tongue. Why couldn't the voice have stuck again before that lovely barb came out?

"Oh, I agree completely." The depth of bitterness in Caroline's tone shook Marge. "And, if you can convince your son of that, we can both get on with our lives." With a flip of shoulder-length honey-blonde hair and a click of one-and-a-half-inch heels, Caroline turned and marched down the sidewalk to her silver Cougar.

Marge closed the door and leaned against it.

"You'll never learn to think before you speak," Gene's voice chided, not for the first time.

"Oh, shut up," Marge retorted. Her face grew hot. What kind of woman tells her dead husband to shut up? A crazy one, probably. What other kind would hear a dead husband talking?

The bigger problem was that Caroline, who had never liked Marge, had even less reason to like her now.

Her mules slapped on the hardwood floor, back down the hallway, a faint echo of Caroline's staccato beat. Catching sight of herself as she approached the full-length mirror at the end of the hall, Marge could understand Caroline's distaste. The face surrounded by unkempt, overgrown curls was drawn. Dark circles and frowning eyebrows framed red-rimmed, dull-green eyes. The wrinkled robe covered a multitude of sins. What was there for Caroline to like?

She leaned forward to get a better look. The bulges beneath the robe were less pronounced than she remembered; the hollows in her face not all from sorrow. Hmmm. Time to check out the scales. Her face softened.

Marge returned to the kitchen. She felt compelled to turn off the radio. The frown came back as unwelcome silence enveloped her. Why should it matter what Caroline thought? She left the music off anyway.

She was seated at the kitchen table with her first cup of coffee before she realized she had put out two mugs and separated the sports and business sections from the newspaper. DAD was imprinted in large letters on one side of the other mug. She drew a sharp breath at the memory of Kate giving it to Gene for his birthday when she was ten years old.

Surely, after a month, she should be used to setting the table for one. Wasn't it time to be getting over it? Caroline was right, she needed to get on with her life. Get back to normal.

Normal what? Gene was gone, dead, leaving her alone, her life empty, after she had arranged the last twenty-seven years to suit him.

"Cut the bull, Marge, my love."

The voice was so clear Marge dropped the paper. She stared at the empty space across from her. Grasping the edge of the table to steady herself, she craned her neck, as if he might be just out of her vision, teasing her. Despite the fact that he wasn't, couldn't be, she narrowed her eyes and shot back, "Well it's true, damn it. I gave you and the kids my life."

"You did it because you wanted to."

"You accepted it willingly enough."

The sound of Gene's laughter was real. The knot of pain under her rib cage tightened until Marge didn't think she could stand it another minute.

"Well, hell, why not? I know when I'm well off."

"How could you?" Marge found herself shouting, her fists clenched as tears coursed down her cheeks. "How could you leave me that way?" She flung the paper across the table into an overwhelming void.

The depth of the silence stopped her. She shrank back against the chair. What if someone saw her yelling at an empty mug? It might be long past time to get over it, but it was certainly not time to go loony.

Marge scowled. What way did Gene leave her?

Suicide, the police said, which didn't make any sense. It would never make sense, no matter what the doctor said about a terminal illness Gene had kept hidden from her. Gene wouldn't do that to her, certainly not to the children. He would have found some way to explain, to say good-bye.

At the very least, he would have made sure everyone understood why suicide was the only solution. He couldn't stand to be thought in the wrong.

She closed her eyes. Her mind once again ran through the details of that morning: waking up and finding herself in bed, alone; padding down to the garage to see if Gene's BMW was missing. He had done that occasionally in the last months of his life, staying out all night without letting her know where he went. He never explained. It was part of the distance that had grown between them. She wanted to confront him, wanted to find out why he felt compelled to seek other companionship. She hadn't dared. It might be the end of the world as she knew it.

The sight of Gene's body slumped over the steering wheel, the sound of the car's motor running—it turned her to stone then and the image was still frozen in her mind now. She couldn't get past that unbelievable sight. She couldn't believe he was gone.

She hadn't told him she was sorry.

Marge could see the strong, square face of the police detective who told her they were closing the case. No matter how many times she told him it couldn't have been suicide, that he had to be wrong, his face was unrelenting, the gray eyes like stone.

"It really couldn't be true, could it?" she whispered. "Did you close yourself up in the garage, turn on the engine of the car, and deliberately desert your family forever?"

"What do you think?" his voice whispered back. A tickling brushed against her ear, as if from Gene's breath. She swept away the sensation and stared at her hand.

"I never meant to push you away," she said in a choked voice. "I never wanted you gone."

At least I never wanted you dead.

It's easy to say I want you back when you're gone forever.

Her hands covered her mouth as she stifled a sob. What if he had guessed? She closed her eyes. "Oh, please, God, please tell me it wasn't my fault," she whispered. No such assurance came; only a tight, cold fear that Gene had sensed her unhappiness, her temptation to fill her empty hours with someone else. Did he kill himself to repay her? Would he kill himself if he were afraid she wouldn't be there for him in his final months?

No. No. No. Not Gene. Not without giving her explicit instructions on how to carry on with her life.

Marge's lips tugged upward in the middle of a sob as she waited for Gene's retort, but he remained silent.

The quiet was broken by the telephone. Marge took a deep breath to steady herself before answering.

"Hello, Mom. How are you this morning?"

Marge felt her tears dry and the band around her heart loosen at the sound of her daughter's voice. "Well, Kate, hello. I think I'm doing okay. How are you? Why aren't you in class?" In her last year of law school, Kate was about to start cramming for final exams.

The telephone magnified the forced quality in Kate's laugh. "I do get a break from classes now and then," she said. "I thought I'd call and see how you were doing. You sound . . . different."

"Everyone seems especially concerned this morning. Robert already sent Caroline around to check on me." Marge cringed at the accusation she heard in her voice. After all, Kate had lost a father. She might have been trying to fill her own need as much as wanting to check on her mother. "How are you doing, darling?"

"As well as possible, I guess. It takes time to get used to, doesn't it? Oh, Mom, I miss him so much. I feel as if . . . as if . . . one of my roots is missing. Does that make any sense?"

Marge started. Kate's words struck a resonating chord in her. "To me it does," she said. "I felt exactly the same way when your grandfather died. My hold on life didn't feel as secure anymore."

Gene's death didn't make Marge feel as if a root was missing. It made her feel as if she had been turned upside down and shaken. Hard.

Kate continued, "I can't imagine you without Dad. It's like you must be a different person if he isn't there with you."

Kate's words brought the furrow back to Marge's brow. "I guess we must have seemed like a unit to you kids. But, I was always a person in my own right, wasn't I?"

If she was a person in her own right, who was she?

This unanswered question was what had driven her life for the last few years. Once the kids were away from home she realized that somewhere in the process of being a wife and a mother she had lost herself. "I guess after marriage I did become part of a *we* instead of a *me*. I have to learn who *me* is all over again."

"You and Dad had such a great marriage," Kate said, as if she hadn't heard. "It was like you were two parts of a whole."

That may have been true once, Marge thought. Not recently though. She wasn't even sure it was a good thing. If it was, where did it go wrong? Why did she end up so lost, so restless?

She shook her head and changed the subject. "Kate, did you notice any difference in your father in the last few months?"

The line was silent for a moment. "Like what? He did seem a little distracted. Sometimes he seemed to be trying too hard to act natural. But, nothing I would have worried about if . . . if he hadn't died."

"Hmmm," was all Marge could respond.

"Have you started making any plans yet?" Kate asked.

"Plans for what?"

"For starting a new life."

"A new life?" She scowled. *A new life?* A vision of the photos and mementos that marked the events of her life being consumed by flames unsettled her. No. That couldn't be right. "I think I'll keep the life I have," she ventured. "I just have to learn how to live it again."

After they ended their conversation, Marge replaced the receiver. Gene seemed to be lurking just beyond every doorway and corner today. The walls crowded in on her. Is this what she had been doing for the last month, hanging around, hoping to catch him unaware, before he could get away again?

Not today.

It was time to get on with her life, remember?

She ran upstairs, pulled a brush hurriedly through her hair, threw on the clothes that came first to hand, grabbed a heavy sweater, and slipped the house keys into her pocket.

Halfway down the driveway she saw Willy Watson emerge from the house next door. "Well, Margy, it's good to see you out and about," he called. "And looking so colorful! Looks like another April shower coming our way, though."

Glancing down, Marge had to grin. Red sweatpants, a yellow shirt, and an old blue sweater of Gene's. Thankfully the only place she had gone since Gene's death was church. What had she worn there? She could only hope she had paid more attention to her attire than she did today.

Raising her eyes, she saw dark clouds closing in on the sun. "I could have chosen a better time," she admitted, but shivered at the thought of going back into that empty house. "But, if I wait for it to be warm and dry in western Washington, I'll never get out."

"Wilma will have something hot waiting for you when you get home," Willy promised her retreating back.

Tears threatened and Marge impatiently swiped at her eyes. Willy and Wilma Watson had been there for her every day for the last month, preparing meals, making sure her needs were met, and giving her company.

She suddenly ached for the calming presence of her best friend, Lori. At least, she thought Lori was her best friend. What kind of a friend made only one appearance in a month? Then again, even the couples that had seemed to be their friends when Gene was alive, as well as the folks from church, stopped visiting after a week or so. They no longer provided any tangible support. She guessed they thought she should be getting over it, too.

But Willy and Wilma were there every day, with hugs and food and encouragement. She didn't know how she would have managed without them. With a wave and a smile, she strode off to test herself on the inclines of Newport Hills.

Detachment enveloped her like a screen, filtering the awakening colors of spring. Marge felt as if she were moving in a different, gray dimension, one filled with emptiness and guilt.

She could barely remember life without Gene. They had met in college, married before they finished, had Robert shortly after graduation, and Kate four years later. Her feet stumbled to a stop. She lifted her face as if seeking something from the newly budded leaves that whispered in the breeze. They seemed to repeat her unanswered questions.

Why was Gene dead?

How had he really died?

"How can I start building a life for myself until I know?" she whispered back.

How would she be able to find answers when the police couldn't?

A large drop of rain spattered her upturned face, cutting her walk short. She hurried back to the house, reaching its dry warmth two minutes before the skies opened in a drenching downpour. Once inside she was at a loss. She looked around helplessly.

Where would she even start?

Five minutes later, Willy and Wilma, huddled under a large umbrella, arrived on the doorstep with a pot of fresh coffee and a plate of warm gingerbread. Willy, round and bald and smooth all over, was covered with a sheen of perspiration despite the cool rain.

Marge welcomed them inside, grateful to put off any further thinking. "Finished your workout for the day?" she asked as she followed the tantalizing aroma into the kitchen. Only Willy's closest neighbors knew his stockiness wasn't all fat. He was almost fanatical about working out with weights in a small gymnasium he had built in one of his two garages.

"You walk, I work out," he answered, flexing an arm muscle. "And Wilma bakes," he added, patting his round stomach.

Willy and Wilma were almost as much of a matched set as their names implied. Both had pale-blue eyes and round, cheery faces. But Wilma's roundness was as soft as Willy's was hard. She looked every bit like the little old lady who baked the gingerbread man as she provided a constant supply of cookies to the neighborhood.

"You must be feeling better," Wilma said when they were seated at the table.

Marge glanced longingly at the gingerbread that was already on its way to her mouth. She put the slice back on her plate.

"I feel almost human again. I need to start figuring out what I'm going to do." She picked up the gingerbread and bit into its spicy sweetness as if to affirm her words.

"Your son has been taking good care of your affairs, I think," Willy said. "You'll be able to pick up and go on without a problem."

Marge winced. Willy was probably right. Robert was a successful accountant who could certainly handle finances, but she didn't like the idea of him taking care of her affairs. She should be able to do that for herself.

I *can* do that for myself.

I *will* do that for myself.

On that resolve, she wolfed down a second huge chunk of gingerbread. As soon as she finished it, she fidgeted in her chair, impatient for the Watsons to leave. Marge needed to be alone so she could plan *how* to do that for herself.

Instead of leaving, Willy took her arm and led her into the dining room. "You know, this was real smart of Gene, putting his desk in the dining room. Makes a real good office without having to trek up and down the stairs, especially since no one does formal dining anymore. Here," he pointed to the desk, "look at the job Robert has been doing for you."

Marge looked at the month's accumulation of mail that was sorted and stacked in neat piles on Gene's oversized mahogany desk. Civic and volunteer information was in a pile on the top left side of the desk, the letters of condolences—opened—were in the middle, and miscellaneous items on the right. Advertising brochures were in the wastebasket. Bills were nowhere to be seen. Under the letters was a small stack of florists cards. "I must go through these," she murmured, her eyes misting. "I've been so remiss. I haven't even thanked anyone for the flowers they sent."

"I know Robert took care of everything," Wilma said from behind. "You don't have to worry about a thing. Come, Willy. I think Marge wants to reread the notes from her friends."

After Marge walked them to the door and said good-bye, she turned and stood in the dining room doorway. The big old desk, Gene's status symbol, loomed in the middle of the room. It was easily the most expensive piece of furniture in the house, purchased at a time when they could ill afford it, but Gene had insisted. Gene was a small man, only an inch taller than Marge's five feet seven inches. He had a thin, wiry build. She always thought the desk made him feel more manly, more powerful.

Why had she never told him she didn't like that big old desk in the middle of the room?

Taking a deep breath she walked into the room, circled the monstrosity, sat in Gene's executive chair, and retrieved her checkbook from the drawer that was her allotted territory.

Only one entry had been added in the last month: a deposit of ten thousand dollars in Robert's handwriting on April 8, 1997. The insurance money, intended to defray the cost of the funeral. Had none of those bills come in yet? She would have to call Robert tonight, when he returned home from work.

Picking up the stack of condolences, she noticed a response date in Robert's bold handwriting. The same notation was on the florists cards. She gazed at them for a moment before picking up a pen. Even if Robert had already responded, this was something she had to do for herself.

She put the pen back down and stared at the telephone with an uneasy feeling in the pit of her stomach. One thing had to be done first. She swallowed hard, grabbed the receiver, and dialed the number for Charles Froyell's law office, half hoping he wouldn't be there. He answered on the second ring.

"Marge, what a pleasant surprise. You sound so much better today." His soft voice caused a fresh onslaught of tears.

"I feel better, thank you," she managed to say, her throat so tight she nearly squeaked. "I believe Gene removed his brother as executor of his will and named you instead. Is that right?"

"Yes, some time ago. He felt that since I had handled his business arrangements I might as well take that over, too. Especially considering . . ."

Yes, Marge knew considering what. Gene's younger brother had lost himself in the bottle many years ago and hadn't been able to stay out of it long enough to handle his own affairs. The surprise was that Gene had taken so long to remove his brother as executor. Maybe he kept hoping the condition was temporary.

"I need to talk with you about whatever arrangements Gene made and what you have done. When can you take time to see me . . . in your office?"

This was business. It had nothing to do with Charles and her.

Charles' voice betrayed surprise and uncertainty when he answered, "But Robert has already met with me several times and has another appointment coming up. I thought he was handling your affairs, Marge. I also thought you and Gene did all the planning together, so you knew what he had done."

They had, until two years ago, when Gene, against Marge's wishes, had opened a new accounting office with Bruce Wilcox. That had been the beginning of the change, the distancing, the secrecy. Marge wasn't sure about anything Gene had done in the last two years.

"Robert has been handling my affairs," she confirmed. "But it's time for me to step in, especially since he doesn't have my power of attorney. I can't imagine what the two of you could have done without that. Why don't I join him when he comes to see you? When will that be?"

"This afternoon at two," Charles replied. "But maybe you should talk to Robert about it first. He is only trying to protect you."

"I'll be there at two," Marge replied. She hung up before Charles could try to talk her out of it.

Feeling good about taking the first step toward getting her affairs in order, Marge settled down with pen and paper. Stamping the second envelope and reaching for a fresh sheet of stationery, she stopped, hand in midair.

Protect her from what?

CHAPTER 2

ROBERT'S SQUARE FACE was framed by neatly trimmed brown hair, which, if allowed to grow a week past his monthly haircut, would shoot wavy tendrils around his ears, much like Marge's auburn curls. Marge suspected it was Caroline who saw to it that this never happened. Robert's dark brown eyes, so like his father's, had the wide, shimmery look Marge remembered from his childhood, when he was determined not to cry after his dog ran into the street and was hit and killed by a car.

When Marge reached up to his nearly six-foot height to plant a kiss on his cheek, it took all her self-control not to wrap him in her arms to comfort him, right in the middle of Charles' office.

"You should have let me handle this," he said, shattering the moment. "You don't know . . ." He shook his head, unable to continue.

Marge glanced into Charles' blue eyes, which were as full of concern as Robert's. She quickly turned away so she wouldn't succumb to the sudden desire to be folded into *his* arms and be comforted. To her relief, Charles made no move to do any such thing.

As if there were nothing but business between them, Charles sat down at his leather-topped desk, where Gene's file lay open in front of him. He hesitated before asking, "Do you know of any change in investment or drain on your assets in the last few months, Marge?"

Marge struggled to draw a breath of air that had suddenly turned dense. She looked directly at Charles. "No," she managed to say.

Charles' carefully manicured fingers ruffled the pages in the folder. When he looked up, his eyes slid past Marge's to focus somewhere over her shoulder. "This is what Robert and I were trying to protect you from until we could figure out what happened. Both the mutual fund and the bond fund were closed about a month before Gene . . . uh . . . died. We can find no trace of the money after the funds were closed."

Momentarily distracted by Charles' stumble over Gene's death, Marge struggled to take in what he had said. Wasn't she a part owner of those investments? Shouldn't Charles have been involved with whatever Gene was doing?

She jumped to her feet and walked to the office door and back again, feeling insecurity growing like an abyss. No money? None?

"Just how did that happen?" Her voice sounded tinny to her ears.

Charles and Robert gazed at Marge; they made her think of small boys waiting for direction. And these men were supposed to take care of her?

Charles managed to speak first. "Well . . . uh . . . it seems you agreed that either one of you could withdraw without the other's signature."

Marge shook her head as she tried to imagine a state of mind that would allow Gene to even think about removing the money without telling her. The agreement was only meant to give one of them easy access to the money if the other was incapacitated.

Head bowed and eyes downcast, Robert said, "Do you think that's why he . . . did it? Because he somehow lost all the money?"

Marge thought for a moment. Her head began to shake back and forth.

"No, no. Don't you see?" she said. "This proves he didn't do it. The only remote possibility of Gene killing himself would have been to avoid using up our resources on his care." She stole a quick glance at Charles, a lightning fast reassessment of what role their incipient dalliance might have played. No, that didn't figure into it at all. It hadn't gone far enough for Gene to be that upset, even if he had suspected something. Besides, to take the money from her was also to take it from the children.

"Gene took his role as provider seriously. There is no way he would lose all our money and then leave me to deal with it." She paused again, thinking about Gene's gradual withdrawal, especially in the last six months, and her concern that he was involved with someone else.

Could he have fallen so hard for someone that he put her care ahead of his family's? No, that didn't compute either. Whatever he might have been doing those last months, Gene was too fair and took his family responsibility too seriously to divert their lifelong savings to a new . . . whatever.

"We don't know for sure the money is lost," Robert said,

though his voice lacked conviction. "We just don't know what he did with it . . . yet."

"But if it is lost . . ." Marge's head whirled. She had to sit down. She leaned forward in the chair, put her head in her hands, and tried to control her thoughts. If the money wasn't lost and Gene planned on killing himself, he would have told her where it was before he died. She looked up. "The fact that the money is missing changes everything. I tried to convince myself it was a bizarre accident, but now . . . now . . ." She stopped. Even though she had never believed Gene killed himself, she had not taken her disbelief to its logical conclusion. Her voice was barely above a whisper when she finished, "I think somebody killed Gene for the money."

"Mother!" Robert cried, jumping to his feet.

"Marge!" Charles expostulated at the same time.

They both stared for a moment, Robert's eyes wide with consternation. "Please, Mother. You're jumping to conclusions. Besides, the police assured us . . ."

"I don't care what the police said," Marge snapped. "They didn't know Gene."

Robert's mouth opened as if he were going to argue with her. He turned to Charles instead.

"What about life insurance? You were going to search for another policy. The funeral policy can't be the only one."

"We didn't need more than that," Marge said.

Robert's breath came out in a strangled huff. "Didn't need . . . Mother, I can't believe Father would leave you without insurance."

"Why not? We carried term insurance on both of us until you and Kate were out of high school, then on Gene until last year, when we knew Kate's law school bills had been paid. We decided it was better to put any additional money into either building the business or adding to our retirement account—which amounted to the same thing."

"I had no idea . . ." Charles' voice trailed off. Marge looked from Charles' dazed eyes to Robert's alarmed ones. Taking term insurance rather than whole life and dropping it when the children were grown was one of the few things she had convinced Gene to do. It seemed to make perfectly good sense, since she would need no more money to live on than the two of them together. Had she been wrong? She shook her head. It still made sense. Their lifetime savings disappearing, that didn't make sense; Gene being dead, that didn't make sense either.

"Is there any way someone else could have accessed our accounts? Or could Gene have used the money to build up the business without thinking to tell me about it?" she asked Charles.

He shook his head. "There is no way to know what he did with the money. When the police investigator first brought this to my attention, I had the broker send me all the documentation relating to the closures. The accounts appear to have been cashed out by Gene, in bank checks made out to him, with no hint of anything irregular about the transactions."

Marge knitted her brow. She couldn't get past the fact that the police knew about the money but still thought Gene had committed suicide. She'd have to talk again to that stubborn detective who handled the case. Evidently no one had adequately explained Gene to him.

"Marge?"

She looked up with a start when she heard Charles' voice. "Is there someone else who knew about the accounts and might have gotten Gene to take the money out for some reason?"

Marge shook her head. "I can't imagine anyone other than Bruce or you."

Charles and Robert exchanged a look Marge couldn't decipher. When neither of them spoke, she continued. "But, if the business needed more money and he took it from our savings, he would have needed you to handle the paperwork, wouldn't he?"

"He should have come to me, yes. That doesn't mean he couldn't do it without telling me, but I don't know why he would. He certainly needed to be sure he was legally covered for any funds he put into the business.

"Anyway, I don't think there is anything in the records that can help us, so we'll have to figure out where to look next. You can leave that to Robert and me. The more urgent problem for you right now is your livelihood. There wasn't much left in Gene's checking or savings accounts. How are you set for your immediate needs?"

"I will take care of my mother," Robert said.

If she hadn't been so close to tears, Marge would have laughed. She remembered Robert's obsessive attentiveness when she helped chaperone a Boy Scout camping trip many years ago. He seemed to fear someone else would step in and protect his mother when that was *his* job. Hadn't his father told him so before they left home?

"I have enough in my personal savings for a couple of months," she said. "By then I will have figured out something. Have you checked on Gene's IRA? Is that money still intact?"

"Yes, it is, and we'll get it rolled over into your IRA as soon as possible. But you shouldn't touch that money if you can avoid it. Not only might you incur stiff penalties, but you still need something for your retirement."

"My retirement!" Marge exclaimed. "My retirement from what? On what?"

As a non-working spouse she deposited only $250 a year in her IRA. Even with growth, it was next to useless. Gene's IRA was better, but it didn't have enough to support her. She would have to get a job.

What kind of job could she get with a rusty applied-arts degree?

Marge still felt dizzy when she returned to her car. She needed to talk with Bruce immediately. She worried for a moment about the look Robert and Charles had exchanged, then sat up straight, relief flooding through her. Bruce and Gene had a partnership agreement. It provided that if one partner died or became incapacitated, the other would buy out his share of the business. When Bruce bought out Gene's share of the business, she might have enough money to live on for several years; maybe . . . maybe enough time to dust off her paints and brushes and put them to good use.

Would Charles have started processing the business insurance already? Why hadn't he mentioned it?

Half an hour later, Marge sat in Bruce's immaculate, tastefully decorated office, staring at Gene's immaculate, tastefully clothed partner, across his spotless desk. Her mouth moved as if to form words, but no sound emerged. She tried again.

"He did *what?*"

"He insisted I buy him out. I had a devil of a time raising the cash, until I found a new partner. That's why it took so long to pay Gene, even though he stopped working three months ago. Meant twice as much work for me, and I was mad as hell until . . . until after it happened. I never said anything because I was sure he had talked it over with you.

Plus, I had the feeling you never really wanted Gene to go into this business anyway."

Marge squirmed. Bruce convinced Gene to join him in a start-up accounting business two years ago. Before that, Marge thought that once their children were grown, Gene and she would take more time for themselves, to travel and enjoy life. She felt betrayed when Gene agreed to join Bruce, leaving the adequate, secure income of his forty-hour-a-week job to take on a position that guaranteed he would have less time to spend with her for the foreseeable future and a less secure income with which to do the enjoying.

"I thought I did a better job of hiding my feelings," she said. "I never had anything against you personally." Marge mentally crossed her fingers. She did hold it against Bruce for talking Gene into the new business venture without caring what was best for Gene and her.

"I know that," Bruce said, with a quick flash of perfect white teeth. He sounded as insincere as Marge felt. "But I already told all this to the police," he added. "They didn't say anything to you?"

"No one has told me anything," Marge said, struggling to control her voice.

Why had no one told her? Charles must have known. Robert probably knew, too.

"Did Gene put any additional money into the business before he sold out?" she asked.

Bruce frowned. "No, there was no need. The business has been doing well. He made a nice little profit when I paid him for his share."

"If he sold out," she mused out loud, "then what did he do with the money? And with our savings?"

Bruce looked up, his eyes sharp. "Your savings? I don't know anything about your savings. And, there is no *if.* He *did* sell." Bruce removed a key from what looked like a green marble paperweight. Opening a burnished wood file cabinet beside his desk, he pulled out a folder.

When the folder fell open, he handed Marge a receipt for three hundred thousand dollars, signed in what certainly appeared to be Gene's handwriting. It included his two hundred and fifty thousand dollar investment in the business plus fifty thousand dollars for the estimated appreciation in value. "It looks like his signature," Marge said, eyes blurring as she struggled to get her thoughts back on track. "But where is the money?"

"Look, I don't know what Gene did with the money. I handed him the check myself. That's all I know."

"Do you have a copy of the check?" Marge asked.

"No. The bank holds check copies for me."

"Did you see the endorsement?"

"No, I never saw it. The police handled whatever needed to be done after Gene died. I understand they were satisfied with their investigation."

Bruce's voice had grown defensive as they talked. Marge's thinking had cleared sufficiently for her to know it was time to change the subject.

"Could I look in Gene's office? In case he left anything there?"

Bruce shook his head. "It's not Gene's office anymore. I had to find a new partner before I could buy Gene out, and he's been in there ever since. Anyway, Gene spent a week going through his office. He made a clean sweep of anything not related to the business."

If Bruce had anything to do with the missing money, he was hiding it well. But who else could it be? When Marge rose to leave, Bruce put his hand out for the receipt. She stood for a moment, staring at Gene's signature. Reluctantly she handed the paper back to Bruce and went to the door. Before closing it, she turned back. "Did Gene say why he was selling?"

"Only that he had made a mistake. You had warned him that it was too much work, and he could finally see you were right. First, it was just that he was tired all the time. Then, when he found out his illness was terminal, he said he wanted to spend the rest of whatever time he had making it up to you." Bruce stopped. His voice had softened. The depth of feeling in it seemed genuine and it triggered Marge's ever-ready wellspring of tears. She was barely able to get out of Bruce's office before they spilled over.

"Gene, Gene, what did you do?" she whispered as soon as she found shelter in the Honda. "What other unpleasant discoveries are in store for me? How many more secrets are Robert and Charles keeping from me? How am I supposed to find out what Bruce . . . or Charles . . . really did?" she wanted to scream. She wanted to cry. She couldn't handle this alone after all.

But she had to. She had no one else.

Clenching her jaw, Marge sat up and turned on the engine. Twenty minutes later she strode back into Charles Froyell's office.

When she burst in, Charles rose and came around his desk, arms outstretched. "Marge, I didn't expect to see you so soon. I'm afraid there hasn't been time to find any further information about what Gene did with the funds he withdrew."

The comfort of Charles' embrace was so tempting Marge sank into it for a moment before pulling back and pounding on his chest.

"Why didn't you tell me? Why are you keeping things from me?" she cried.

"What?" Charles stumbled back a step. "What are you talking about?"

Marge turned away and took a deep breath to regain her composure. "Actually, I've been trying to think of one good reason why I should continue using you as my attorney."

Charles' head snapped back. "What have I done? I've only tried to help you in any way I can. You can't blame me for what Gene did."

"You don't consider failing to tell me that Gene sold his half of the business and allowing me to go and face Bruce without that knowledge is grounds for dismissal?"

Surprise widened Charles' eyes. "You went . . . well . . . you're right. That was . . . inconsiderate, and I apologize," he stuttered. "I did want to tell you earlier, but it seemed like you had been hit with too much already." He gave her a look of accusation and his voice became indignant. "I didn't expect you to go charging off to see Bruce without telling me first. You should trust me to handle things. I don't know why Gene sold the business, but I guess we should have figured he would, considering everything else."

Marge glared at him. "Considering *what*?"

Charles faced Marge and grasped her hands. "I shouldn't have said anything. I don't want to upset you more, and I don't like to speak ill of the dead, but it's pretty obvious something was going on that Gene didn't want to tell you about. Something he needed the money for. You thought he was up to something, too. Otherwise, why would you have . . ." He stopped, released her, and stepped away to pull out his pipe, look at it for a moment, and put it back in his pocket.

Marge took a deep breath. "I think our relationship was a mistake, Charles. And even if it wasn't, I don't know how we could continue it." Especially when you might be the one who caused Gene's death, she thought. No one else had such access to all their finances. "Since our history will make things awkward between us, I think we should also end our business relationship."

"You're feeling guilty about us because Gene died," Charles said, the gentleness of his voice making Marge's resolve waver. "That doesn't change how things were between you two before he died, and it doesn't have to change anything between us in the future. I can wait until you sort it out for yourself."

Marge rubbed her forehead in consternation. Maybe Charles was right. She certainly had no reason, except confusion and frustration, to think he had something to hide. At any rate, she didn't have to decide anything right now. And she was far too tired and too unsure of her feelings to argue about it.

"So, you didn't handle the buyout?" Her voice sounded as flat as she felt.

"No. Gene did it without telling me. I suppose he thought there was no threat to his interests so he didn't need a lawyer. The first I knew about it was when the police were looking into Gene's business. As far as I know, they never discovered what he did with that money either. It wasn't deposited in any account that we know about."

"Why would the police check his finances, I wonder, if they already figured he had committed suicide?"

Charles grinned. "It seems a certain lady wasn't too happy with their investigation and demanded they find out what really happened. So, they decided to see if someone benefited financially from his death. But since it appeared Gene lost the money, it gave them one more reason to conclude that he committed suicide. I believe they let it go at that."

He pulled his pipe out again and leaned back on the sofa. "Perhaps you should also accept that, Marge. Concentrate on planning your future and getting your finances in order."

Marge just shook her head.

"Speaking of finances," she said, "it occurred to me that Gene received checks when he cashed out our funds. If he didn't deposit those checks into an account, he would have had to endorse them over to someone. Have you contacted the fund's bank to see who he endorsed them to?"

Charles stared at her. "Are you sure you didn't go to law school?" he asked with a smile. "No, we haven't gotten that far yet." ·

"Is there any way, if Bruce doesn't cooperate, that we can get a look at the buyout check? For the same reason?"

"I'll look into it," he said. "Enough business. Is there anything I can do for you? Would you like a glass of wine?" He glanced at his watch. "It's after five. Why don't we have a nice early dinner, to end your hard day on a pleasant note?"

Marge turned to the door. "No, Charles. I think I need to be alone. It has been a long day." Alone was the last thing Marge wanted to be, but she didn't know if she could handle being with Charles, either, with doubts about him clouding her feelings.

"You have to eat some time, and if you let me take you out, you won't have to cook when you get home."

Marge wouldn't have to cook anyway. Wilma would have something for her. Another macaroni dish? Or a tuna casserole? Suddenly dinner out sounded like a pretty good idea. She'd have to apologize to Wilma, but it'd be worth it.

"Oh, all right. As poor as I am beginning to feel, I guess I shouldn't pass up a free meal."

In the elevator to the parking garage, Marge noted Charles' studiedly casual appearance, from the long graying sideburns in his otherwise medium-brown hair to a tweed jacket with leather sleeve patches. The aroma of sweet pipe tobacco completed a package that undoubtedly brought confidence and comfort to many clients.

Comfort would feel pretty good at the moment; unfortunately, she couldn't afford to wallow in it with Charles.

They took Charles' car the short distance to the restaurant, leaving hers parked in the garage. The staff in the restaurant greeted Charles as if they knew him. Marge looked around. Dim lighting that gave off a rosy glow to the restaurant and plush furnishings testified to the expense of the menu.

"Would you like a drink? A glass of wine?" he asked.

Marge wanted to avoid the encroaching lethargy brought on by her surroundings and shook her head.

When the waiter had taken their order and departed, Charles reached over and covered her hand with his. "I want you to remember I am here for you, Marge," he said. "No matter how long it takes you to get over your loss, even if you decide we don't have any closer relationship, I am your friend. I care very much about what happens to you."

Marge became still and stared at his hand on top of hers. Confusion filled her when she thought about Charles, what almost was, what might be in the future. Guilt followed on top of the confusion. She couldn't handle it now. She had to be cool, uninvolved, at least until she sorted out what Gene had done in the last months of his life and she knew who had taken their money and killed him. As if sensing her discomfort, Charles removed his hand and took a sip of the wine he had ordered for himself.

Crumbling a piece of dinner roll, Marge switched subjects to see if she could catch Charles off guard. "Charles, how did Gene manage to do all this stuff without you, his attorney, having a clue? Or did you really know but you don't want to admit it?"

"Marge, how can you think such a thing? Of course I didn't know. Gene didn't have to clear anything with me. I'm surprised he didn't involve me in the buyout of the business. If nothing else, he could have put himself in some tax trouble; though as an accountant, I suppose he figured he could take care of the details. I'm as much in the dark as you are."

"Tax trouble? Am I going to be in trouble with the IRS, since Gene sold everything at a profit?"

"No, no. You let me handle that. You have a huge loss, remember? With all the police corroboration we have, there will be no problem with the IRS. Unless, of course, we recover the money, in which case I think you'll welcome whatever problems might surface."

Marge nibbled on her oriental chicken salad. She had little appetite and nervously looked up every time someone walked into the restaurant. Charles' answers seemed open and honest. So did Bruce's. How would she know if they weren't?

"Marge, you don't have to be afraid someone will see us," Charles finally said. "You are having a business dinner with your lawyer. Besides, you aren't married anymore."

"No one would know you're my lawyer, Charles. Anyway, it's too soon." She sighed. What did she think she was going to learn over dinner with Charles? She didn't even know what questions to ask. "This was a mistake, just like all the times we met before Gene died."

Charles put down a forkful of salmon and reached across the table to take her hand again. "Gene never knew we met. And we never did anything wrong, though I'm not sure we can say the same for Gene. You have no reason to feel guilty."

Marge wanted to believe him. She also wanted to believe Gene hadn't had an affair. But, if he hadn't, and if he didn't suspect her, what did he do with the money? And how did he spend his time before he died?

It was nearly seven o'clock when they finished eating and the waiter returned with the box of leftover salad she had requested.

"I really must finish some things this evening," she said, standing.

Charles glanced at his watch and hurried to pay the check, as if he had been unaware of the time passing. "It has been such a pleasure being with you, Marge, away from all the worries for a while. I hope it was a nice break for you, too."

His voice sounded strained. Marge regretted the accusation he must have heard in her words, but she had to get to the truth—and Charles hadn't helped her do that. She had accomplished nothing this evening except to get a free meal and probably ruin a relationship that held a lot of promise.

As soon as she was alone, her mind again flooded with doubt. How could Charles know so little about what was going on in Gene's business and finances? Didn't he hold important papers and handle Gene's legal affairs? Could Charles possibly have had something to do with the money disappearing . . . or with Gene's death?

When Marge entertained the thought that Charles could have been wooing her while planning Gene's murder she felt a sudden need for that glass of wine.

As soon as she was in the house, Marge went to the cabinet Gene used as a bar and pulled out a bottle of Merlot, uncorked it, and poured a glass with shaking hands. She and

Gene often had a drink before dinner—she drank wine and he usually chose Scotch. She had never had a glass of wine when she was alone. How many things would she have to learn to do by herself or give up? She certainly didn't intend to give up the things she enjoyed.

Taking the wine with her, Marge went to Gene's desk and found his checkbook. There was no entry for the three hundred thousand dollars he got from Bruce. Did he have another account that Charles might not know about? A search of the desk turned up no evidence of one. Either he had an account hidden somewhere or he endorsed the check directly over to a third party.

Who could the third party be? If Gene signed over the check to someone and the police had checked Bruce's account, as Bruce indicated they did, then they must know how the check was endorsed. Would they give her that information? Had they told Robert or Charles? And, were Robert and Charles still holding out on her?

Marge sat back and pulled at a lock of hair in bewilderment. Bruce had no access to their savings funds except through Gene. Charles had no access to the business money except through Gene. But anyone, including one of them, could have convinced or coerced Gene to withdraw the funds and entrust them with the money, then killed him later to cover their tracks. Had one of his most trusted associates done it? If so, which one?

She sighed. Charles was right about one thing. It was hard to concentrate on what happened when she didn't know how she was going to support herself. Once the funeral expenses were paid, the ten thousand in her account would be next to nothing. By next month she wouldn't have enough money to buy groceries.

"Don't forget the BMW."

Marge sat up straight. "What?" Where had that come from? What about the BMW?

With a swift slap to her head, Marge realized the BMW was the quickest source of money she had. Selling it would give her what she needed to live on for maybe a year. Thank God Gene had insisted he needed a luxury car for his business. It was all she had going for her now.

Marge's fingers began to itch. She climbed up into the attic and rummaged through the hodgepodge of items that had accumulated in the last twenty-four years to find her art supplies. Taking them down to the second floor, she stowed them in the closet of Robert's old bedroom. She was too tired and distracted to do anything with them tonight, but the tingling told her the long drought was over. Tomorrow she would do something.

CHAPTER 3

A QUICK TRIP TO the Newport Hills Public Library in the morning established the book value on the BMW at $22,000. It was less than half their past annual income, but Marge was sure she could make it stretch for a year, especially if she found a part-time job.

Pulling into the driveway at home, she stared for a long time at the closed garage door. She glanced at Wilma and Willy's house, as if looking for support. Closing her eyes and taking a deep breath, she hit the remote, stepped out of the Honda, squared her shoulders, and marched forward. As the garage door rolled up, she took another deep breath and walked inside.

An overpowering smell of exhaust fumes hit her hard. She stumbled back. Memory of the sight of Gene slumped at the wheel of the BMW made her stomach lurch.

"You okay, Margy?"

Marge opened her eyes and reached out for the firm support Willy offered.

"You should have called me before trying this," he scolded. "Why don't you come on over and let Wilma fix you a cup of coffee?"

"No . . . no, thank you, Willy," she said, her voice shaking. "I have to get this over with. I have to be able to get into the car and sell it."

"You don't need to bother yourself about something like that. I'd be glad to handle it for you. Why, Wilma and I don't have anything else to do but help our neighbors, now that we're retired."

Marge smiled. Willy's patter calmed her nerves and settled her stomach. "Willy, thank you so much for being here for me. But, this is something I have to do for myself. After all, I have to learn to do things for myself, don't I?"

Willy argued and grumbled, but finally let go of Marge's arm. To Marge's relief he stayed where he was while she went into the garage and peered through the windows of the car. There were no strong fumes, of course, just a lingering trace of the odor that seemed to hover menacingly in the air. That was the only indication of the tragedy in which the car had played such a central role.

"Wilma's making a tuna casserole for your lunch," Willy said when she turned back to him.

"Oh, no. Tell her not to do that. I'm going to be busy all day and I don't know when or where I'll grab lunch."

"Well, we'll plan on something for dinner then. I know Wilma will want to hear all about your busy day. It's so good to have you out and about again."

The phone was ringing when she walked in the door.

"Mother, where have you been? I've been worried sick,

not able to reach you yesterday afternoon and then again this morning."

"Kate, I'm sorry. I got tired of sitting at home feeling blue and decided to start living again. There is so much to do, and I have so much to tell you."

"Yes, Robert has already told me some of it. I can't believe it. No money! What could Dad have done?"

"That's what I'm going to find out. And also what happened to him."

"Well, I agree with you about Dad. I never did think he could be so inconsiderate as to commit suicide. But I don't know what you can do about it. Have you talked to the police?"

"And tell them what? I thought about it, but I realized all I could tell them was that I knew my husband better than they did, and I know he wouldn't kill himself. Unless I can find something new, they won't have any reason to reopen the case. They already know he sold the business, and they seem to have checked his finances pretty thoroughly."

Kate gasped. "Sold the business? When did he do that?"

"About two months ago. And he never told me, either. Nor did Charles or Robert. I had to find it out for myself." After pausing a moment to stem the rising anger, she continued, "Do you know Bruce Wilcox at all?"

"I only met him once or twice, so I don't have any opinion about him. Why? Do you think he's lying?"

"I don't know. I have no reason to distrust him, and I don't know how he could get access to our savings, but I don't think I should trust anyone right now. I'm sure it was your father's signature on the receipt. I suppose that money went into the same hole our savings did."

"Let me see what I can find out about him from the

county records. At least I should be able to locate the partnership change, if Bruce is being truthful. Dad was too smart to get into anything without all the legal angles covered.

"But, Mom. How are you going to live? If only I were working instead of finishing my last year of school." She paused. Her voice was thoughtful when she continued. "Although, I'll be working as soon as I graduate. That's why I was trying to reach you. I got the position at Wilkinson and Miller. And, you know, it would be an easy commute if I came home to live."

"Congratulations, darling! I know having that settled is a load off your mind. But, let's not make any hasty decisions. You have your own life to live, too. I'm going to sell the BMW and that should give me enough money for at least a year. By then we should either have found the money or I should have a job."

After a short silence, Kate said, "I'm not sure you should live alone, Mom. And I don't think that money will go very far. Think about it, but don't take too long. If I have to rent an apartment in town, I'll need to make arrangements fairly soon. Can you get someone else to sell the car? I know I never want to see it again."

Marge ignored the implication that she couldn't live by herself. Still, she did need to evaluate her future financial needs. When she was in college she had visions of being a starving artist, but at forty-seven years of age she wasn't sure she was ready to subsist on beans, especially since she now had much less confidence in the commercial prospects of her work.

But Marge knew she could handle selling the BMW. "The worst is over with," she told Kate. "I made myself look at the car today."

As soon as they said good-bye and Marge hung up the phone, it rang again. "You okay, Mom?" Robert asked. "I thought you were going home from Charles' office yesterday. You had us worried when you weren't home later."

"I'm fine, Robert," she said with a sigh. *Are my children to become my keepers?* "Don't expect me to be home all day any more. I have too many things to do."

"I wish you'd let me help. I know Dad would want me to take care of you."

"I need to learn to take care of myself, Robert." She stopped, took a breath to steady herself, and spoke slowly to keep her voice from shaking. "Does taking care of me include not telling me that your father sold his share in the accounting business in addition to losing our life's savings?"

The line was silent.

"Robert? Are you still there?"

"It seemed like the best thing to do. I didn't think you could handle any more after Dad died, so I convinced the police to not bother you with it. Then, yesterday, when you were so upset about the funds, I couldn't find the courage to tell you. I'm sorry. That's why I phoned, but I couldn't reach you. I certainly didn't think you would go see Bruce by yourself . . ."

"Enough, Robert. Enough." Marge's anger evaporated, leaving her deflated. "When did you find out your father was selling his share of the business?"

"When the police told us. Father never told me anything. More unusual is that he didn't tell Charles either."

Marge shook her head to try and clear the confusion. If Gene had told anyone other than herself or Charles it would have been Robert. Why hadn't he told anyone? "Are there any more secrets you've kept from me?" she asked. "Like the house doesn't belong to me, or the cars?"

"Please, Mother! There's nothing else. Are you sure you're okay after all this? I could send Caroline over to spend the day."

"Oh, I'm sure she'd like that, Robert," Marge said grimly. "But why don't you do the honors instead?"

The line was silent again. "Well, uh, if you really need me, I guess I could manage it. It's easier for Caroline; though she did mention you weren't that cordial yesterday."

Marge sighed. Sarcasm was lost on her son. "No, Robert. I don't need anyone to come over. I won't be home much anyway." She paused. "Bruce told me the police investigated and were satisfied with the buyout. Did you see a copy of the check?"

"No, they didn't show it to me. Why?"

"Your father didn't put the money in our account. Either he has another account or he endorsed it over to someone else. How can I get a look at the check?"

"I can ask the police. But what difference will it make?"

Duh! Was this really her sharp accountant son?

"Whoever he endorsed it over to might know where the money is. Or it might be the person who stole the money and killed your father. I'll ask the police myself. I need to talk to them anyway."

"Mother, please. Don't pursue your ideas about Dad's death. The police know what they're doing, and they decided it was suicide."

Marge thought it was just as well not to tell Robert she planned to pursue her ideas until the police changed their minds. "Well, I'll just look at that check and see who it was endorsed to. Then maybe we can find the money. Oh, by the way, I want an accounting of all the bills you paid for me so I can pay you back."

"You don't need to . . . Well, we should probably get together and talk about everything. I've had some thoughts about the future. Why don't Caroline and I come over tonight? Don't make dinner, we'll bring Chinese food."

Marge's brow creased. What kind of thoughts was Robert having about her future? Guess she'd better find out sooner rather than later.

"All right. I'll see the two of you around five-thirty." At least their company would mean not being alone in the house another evening. Or having tuna casserole. She called Wilma to let her know the change in plans.

Next she phoned the police station. "I'd like to speak to Detective Pete Peterson, please."

"I'm sorry, he's not available. Can I take a message?"

"Please ask him to call Marge Christensen—unless there is someone else involved with my husband's death who can help me."

"No, Detective Peterson would be the one involved in any death. I'll tell him you called."

Marge gave her number and hung up. She remembered waiting for return calls several times in the last month. She supposed police detectives were always busy, even in a city as quiet as Bellevue, Washington.

Marge sat for a few minutes, staring at the phone. She wanted to concentrate on finding out what happened to Gene and to the money. Unfortunately, little things like groceries and utilities and house repairs would not wait until she had satisfied that need.

Since the idea had popped into her head, she decided to make sure the house was still hers, and then transfer the title on it and anything else she and Gene had jointly owned into her name only. Which wouldn't amount to much any more.

Marge pulled out the phone book to find numbers and make appointment at an employment agency and the Bellevue BMW dealership.

As she pulled the BMW out of the garage and headed to town, the odor stayed with her, making the back of her neck tingle. The first stop was at HairMasters on Coal Creek Parkway, no appointment needed. She had to take care of the mop on her head before she could face anyone.

Next stop, the employment agency. Marge left feeling deflated. While they would keep her application on file, they recommended she enroll with a temporary agency to get some work experience. What had she expected? That a job would magically appear for an unskilled housewife twenty-five years out of college? The BMW money would have to last a long, long time.

Northrup Way and the BMW dealership were just down the road a bit. After she parked in the lot, Marge sat in the car for a moment, trying to recapture the confidence she had felt before she left the house. It was impossible.

"Why did you do this to me, Gene?" she asked, pounding on the steering wheel. "Why did you leave me alone to handle the consequences of what you did?"

But he didn't. She felt a wave of guilt for her anger. He didn't go of his own accord.

"Mrs. Christensen, my name is Paul Hendricks," the manager said when a salesman ushered her into his office. "I was so saddened to hear about your loss. Please, let me know how I can help you."

Marge had to clear her throat before she could make her voice audible. "I plan to sell the BMW," she said. "I'd like to know what kind of a price I can get for it."

The manager sat back and pursed his lips. "Did Mr.

Christensen tell you he was considering selling the car?" Marge's head jerked up. "I see he didn't. He came by before he died and asked what we would give him for it."

"When was that? Did he say why?"

"Let's see." He flipped back the pages of his calendar. "That must have been about eight or nine weeks ago. He didn't say why. When I gave him the price we could pay, he said he'd come back and let me know in a couple of weeks."

"What did you offer him?" She asked.

"Full wholesale value. Even without checking, we knew the car was in good condition because Mr. Christensen always brought it in for every little squeak."

Marge rubbed at the knot forming between her brows. Less than three months ago Gene had received the final results of his medical tests. Was he planning to sell the car because he was dying and wouldn't need it? Or would that money have followed their savings into the black hole?

"Is there any way I can get more than wholesale value?" she asked. "I need as much money as I can get."

Paul narrowed his eyes in thought. "In normal circumstances, you could sell it yourself and get close to book value—up to two thousand more than wholesale. Of course, you have to be willing to deal with the negative side of selling it yourself. Unfortunately, that's not your worst problem."

"Well, first, what are the negatives of selling it myself?" Marge asked.

"Your ad with your home phone number will be published in the paper. Who knows what kinds of calls you will get? Or what sort of people will say they are coming over to look at the car in order to get your address? Plus, it is a hassle dealing with all the calls."

"I've been through that once before," Marge said with a grin. "Though that was many years ago. So, what is the worst problem?"

Paul hesitated, seemed to be searching for the right words. "The car's history," he finally said. "Let's look at the car before we go any further."

After checking the car over and returning to his office, Paul continued. "You must have noticed the odor in the car. It will be hard to get rid of. If you don't, most people will be turned off or at least demand you lower the price. Even without the odor, this is a small community and your husband's death was big news. People will know what happened and why you're selling. You also need to have it checked for engine damage from running in idle that length of time."

Marge didn't realize she had been holding her breath until it came out in a rush. "Wow," she managed once she could make her voice work. "I'm going to have to think this through. Will you still take it, if I want to sell it to you?"

"Yes, of course we will. Mr. Christensen was a good customer and a friend. We'll do whatever we can to help you. But, we will have to run engine diagnostics and determine how much cleaning it needs before we'll know what we can offer you."

Marge stood. "Thank you so much for your time and for being up front about everything."

Marge nearly stumbled on her way back to the car. Inhaling deeply, she turned on the ignition. Whatever value the dealer put on the car, she should be able to get one or two thousand more if she sold it herself. In her present financial position she had no choice.

Should she be thankful that Gene had died before he could finish carrying out his plan to sell the BMW and possibly lose that money, too? She shuddered. That was unthinkable.

Stopping at the bank on the way home she fidgeted for fifteen minutes waiting to see an account representative. When she was ushered into the office it took only two minutes to determine that no changes had been made to the mortgage or ownership of the house. She could return with a copy of the death certificate and get everything put in her name alone.

As she headed out to the car, her step felt light. She shook her head. It was a sad state of affairs when she was elated to find out she still owned what she knew she owned three months ago.

As soon as she entered the house, without giving herself time for doubt to creep in, she wrote an ad for selling the BMW and called it in to the *Bellevue Journal American*. Next she began to search for temporary employment agencies. While she was deciding which agency to contact, the phone rang.

"Pete Peterson here. You had a question?" Marge had forgotten how curt he could be.

"Yes, Detective Peterson. Did you get a copy of the check Bruce Wilcox paid my husband when he bought out the business? Or the checks Gene received for our investment funds? I need to find out how those checks were endorsed."

A deep sigh came over the line. "Call me, Pete, please. I don't remember getting a copy of the checks, but I'll look in the files to be sure."

"Don't you think you should have done that before closing the case on his death? If you knew my husband, you'd know he wouldn't commit suicide for any of the reasons you've come up with yet. I suspect you're trying to make sure Bellevue has another year without a homicide on the books."

His voice was hard now. "We thoroughly investigated your husband's death, Mrs. Christensen. There is no evidence that it was anything other than suicide."

Marge's voice was as cold as the detective's when she answered. "Thank you for looking up those checks for me. You'll be hearing from me again."

"I'm sure I will," she heard him mutter.

The doorbell rang. She opened it to find Willy and Wilma with a tuna casserole for all three of them. She pushed aside irritation at the delay in her plans and forced a smile.

"She won't take no for an answer," Willy said with a grin.

"Willy tells me you're going to sell Gene's car." Wilma, as usual, entered talking. She bustled past Marge and put the casserole on the table. Without pausing for breath she started pulling plates out of the cupboard. "I'm glad to hear it. You need to get that reminder out of your life."

"I also need the money," Marge said, setting out silverware and filling water glasses before Wilma could do all of the work.

Willy looked up from his favorite spot in Marge's house, her rocking chair, where he was rocking gently. "Isn't the life insurance here yet? That's pretty poor service."

"We didn't have life insurance," Marge explained once again. "Or rather, just enough to cover funeral expenses."

The room was suddenly silent as Wilma's bustling and Willy's rocking stopped at the same time.

Wilma broke the silence. "But, that's terrible," she said. "How could Gene take a chance like that? My Willy would never . . ." She broke off, as if realizing that wasn't the most comforting thing to say and reached out to put her arms around Marge. "You poor, poor dear."

"I'm going to sell the BMW and get a job," Marge said as she momentarily succumbed to the consolation, sudden misgivings making her legs feel weak. She resolutely pulled away. "I'll be fine, don't worry."

Willy started to rock slowly, concern clouding his face. Wilma put the finishing touches on lunch and they sat down to eat. When they had finished and the dishes were cleared away, Marge took a deep breath.

"Willy, Wilma, you two have been absolute rocks this past month. I don't know what I would have done without you. But, I'm better now. You must stop doing so much for me or I will feel guilty for taking advantage of you."

"You don't need to feel guilty for anything," Wilma said with a wave of her hand. "We're glad to do it, and we're glad to do anything more we can to help. You aren't over it yet. You may feel better today, but who knows how you'll feel tomorrow? We aren't going to abandon you like some of your friends have. Don't forget that we're right next door if you need anything," were her parting words as they left.

Leaving the BMW in the driveway, Marge used the Honda to drive to the temporary employment agency.

"What kind of work are you looking for?" asked the representative.

"I don't know," Marge said, explaining her background again.

"Well, would you prefer office or retail? Short-term or long-term?"

Marge had no idea what she preferred. She sighed. So many decisions to make. "What do you consider short-term?"

"Two weeks or less."

Marge pressed her hands against the sides of her head. Her life was too uncertain to take on a long-term engagement. She surprised herself by leaving the office clutching her copy of the signed agreement.

Turning in at the driveway Marge hesitated before parking the Honda in the garage, leaving the BMW outside. The BMW needed a thorough cleaning, and the garage did, too. She entered the house through the kitchen door, rubbed her eyes, and stretched, feeling the day's tension in every muscle of her body. She went upstairs for a shower, letting slightly cool water flow over her in a refreshing stream. She dressed in comfortable slacks and a sweatshirt and surveyed herself in the mirror.

No, this would not do. She needed something to bring her a little closer to Caroline's crisp appearance. Rummaging through the closet, she came up with dress slacks and a tailored blouse, ran an iron over them both, and changed clothes. She brushed her clipped but still errant curls into an auburn halo around her face. Much better.

"I see you have the BMW out," Robert said when he and Caroline came in shortly after five-thirty. "Are you going to drive it now?"

"No, I'm going to sell it," Marge replied.

"But, why? Oh, well, I guess you wouldn't want to drive it after what happened. It's a shame, though."

He looked so wistful Marge couldn't help thinking of when Gene bought the car. He had come up with all sorts of rationalizations for why a BMW would be good for business. It would give him the successful image that would breed confidence in his customers, he had said. But it was the yearning look on Gene's face that sold Marge. She knew the car was more for his ego than anything else, but if his ego needed it she didn't see why he shouldn't have it. She wished she could afford to give the car to Robert.

"Really, Robert. How could you ever drive it?" Caroline asked from the kitchen, where she was arranging cartons of Chinese food. "It would give me the shivers to even sit in it."

Marge felt a flash of the same guilt she saw on Robert's face. "Actually, I did drive it today," she admitted, leading Robert to the kitchen to join Caroline. "It wasn't easy, but I had to take it to the dealer to find out what he would pay for it."

"So, did you sell it?" Robert asked.

"No, he would only give me wholesale value for it, probably less actually, because of any odor or mechanical damage they would have to fix. If I sell it myself I can get more; though I'll still have to discount it because of what happened. I put an ad in the paper today."

"Mother, you amaze me. I never would have thought you would do something like that by yourself."

Marge glanced up from setting the table in time to see the look of disgust Caroline threw at him. For once she had to agree with Caroline.

"You should get some help selling the car. I mean, you don't have any experience with these things," Robert continued.

"I've sold a car before."

"Really? When?"

"You were a toddler and your father took a bus to work. I was expecting again and we couldn't afford to keep two cars. We decided to sell the one I had before we were married." Marge sat down at the table, smiling at the memory of two young people so full of life and future hopes. "I put

47

an ad in the paper. The next day the phone started ringing and it didn't stop for three days, even though I sold the car the first day." With a shake of her head she came back to the present. "I'm glad I remembered that. I'll have to call the Department of Motor Vehicles and make sure I know the current requirements for changing ownership. I think I'll also cancel the voice mail and hook up the phone and answering machine your father brought home from the office. It'll be easier to manage the calls." She stopped. "I always did wonder why he brought that home. He didn't tell me why, just put it up on a closet shelf where I found it when I was cleaning. How did he figure I wouldn't call him at work after he sold out?"

"You never phoned Father at work, unless it was an emergency," Robert reminded her. "I remember how you scolded me whenever I called him about some trifling thing that could have waited until he got home."

Marge nodded. "And he always called me at least once a day when he had a chance. He started calling two or three times a day the last couple of months, but he hardly had anything to say. I guess he didn't want to take any chances that I might have a reason to phone." She shook her head again. She didn't want to admit she had suspected Gene might be checking up on her. "I don't understand how I could not have known something was wrong. I was so busy feeling sorry for myself for not doing all the things I wanted to with my life that I missed the signs he must have been giving . . . what could he have been doing with his days for two months?"

She looked up in time to see Robert catch a sharp look from Caroline. So they think Gene was up to something I shouldn't find out about, too, she thought. Is there still more they know but are hiding from me?

The phone rang, breaking the awkward silence.

"Pete Peterson here. I have that information you asked me for earlier."

"Yes, detective. Who was the check endorsed to?"

"Call me Pete," he said. "We didn't get a copy of that check. Mr. Wilcox didn't give his permission. Since your husband committed suicide, there was no reason to pursue it further. But the checks from cashing out your other accounts were endorsed to something called the Cheltington Investment Company."

Marge wrote the name while Robert looked over her shoulder. "Did you investigate to find out what it was?"

"No. There was no reason to. He invested the money. You should be able to get it put in your name, if he didn't already do that."

"First, I have to find the investment," Marge said dryly. "It would have helped if you had completed the job."

"Good-bye, Mrs. Christensen."

Marge stared at the telephone. "I think he just hung up on me," she said and slowly replaced the receiver. "I thought Bruce said the police had looked at the check." She frowned in concentration. "No . . . no, he didn't. He said the police had investigated and were satisfied. He never specified what they had investigated. I wonder why he was so evasive?"

Robert shook his head. "Mother, you're going to drive yourself crazy if you don't let it go. The police said Father committed suicide. Forget it. Go on with your life. I'll look up this company and see what I can find out about the investment. You may end up in good financial shape after all."

Angry at Robert's ability to accept the police verdict so easily, Marge turned to help Caroline stow the leftover Chinese food and clear the dishes from the table. Once they had finished, Robert asked them to sit back down at the table. "I want both of you together to talk about this," he said. "I have an idea that I think solves a lot of problems for all of us."

Marge looked at Robert, then Caroline, alarmed. Caroline's puzzled look confirmed her fears. "Robert, you should talk this over with Caroline first, whatever it is . . ."

"No," Robert interrupted. "I don't think this can wait." He took a deep breath, glanced quickly at Caroline, and said, "I think Caroline and I should give up our apartment and move in here. We could make some arrangement to buy the house, so you would have your own money, Mother. And with both of us working, you could keep the house running, and . . ." he held up his hand and rushed on as Caroline seemed ready to break in. ". . . and Caroline doesn't want to quit work to have a family, so I thought . . . I thought . . ."

He couldn't ignore Caroline's indignation any longer. "Your mother was right," she said, her voice icy and quiet. "You should have discussed this with me first."

"You've always said you needed help with the housework," Robert began, but Caroline didn't let him continue.

"I always said I needed *you* to help me with the housework," she said in the same tight voice. "But your mother evidently taught you that was woman's work. And, *if* I decide I want to have a child, it will be because *I* want to raise it. It would be nice to say *we* could raise it, but I'm beginning to understand that might be too much to hope for. Your mother probably taught you that also was a woman's responsibility. You've been trying all your life to be your father. Taking his place in this house would do the trick, wouldn't it? You could stop badgering me to be your mother because you'd have your very own mother right here at your beck and call. Well, fine. Move in with your mother. Be lord of the manor. But count me out. I'll send your clothes over."

"Caroline, wait . . ." Robert called, but Caroline was already out the door.

"Go after her, Robert," Marge said.

"She won't listen . . ."

"Go after her, Robert, because you aren't staying here."

CHAPTER 4

～

Marge followed Robert as he ran out the front door. They caught the squeal of Caroline's tires as she backed out of the driveway and sped away. Robert stood still, staring after the car, his face as forlorn as an abandoned little boy's.

"Robert, what is going on?" Marge asked as she took his arm and led him back into the house. "That didn't sound like something new."

"We've been arguing for months about starting a family, about who should do what, about everything you can imagine," Robert said in a dispirited voice. "You and Dad never had these problems. I thought if we moved in here, she could learn something from you about how marriage works. About how to be a wife."

Marge winced. Had giving up her art and dedicating herself to her children been a bad thing? She shook her head; she had done what she wanted to do. If Caroline or Kate didn't want to live that way no one should fault them for it. Not even Robert. An uneasy feeling crept through her. How much of her discomfort with Caroline was because Caroline had chosen a different path than her? How much of Caroline's dislike stemmed from Marge's own attitude?

"Robert, there is no one way to be a wife," she said as she stood beside his chair and ran a hand through his short curls—the way she had when he was a teenager, depressed because life wouldn't mold itself to suit his needs. Maybe he was born that way. Maybe it wasn't her fault. "There is no one way for a marriage to work. It's all a matter of choices, choices you make over and over again. I made a choice to stay home and be a homemaker. Most of the time I was happy with that decision, and I tried hard not to show it when I wasn't. For me, watching you and Kate grow up was the most rewarding thing I could do. If I had realized it might distort your view of what marriage should be, I might have taken the risk of doing something different."

"Well, it doesn't make any difference now." Robert's shoulders slumped. "My marriage is finished. I guess I was grasping at straws, but I convinced myself this could work.

"I still don't understand why it can't. You need us, we need you. Isn't that what family is all about? But Caroline has to have it all her way. She doesn't care how unhappy I am."

"Is Caroline responsible for your happiness?" Marge mused, realizing for the first time how much she had relied on Gene and the kids for her own.

"She doesn't think so," Robert said, his voice bitter. "All we ever talk about are her and her needs. You'd think I didn't have any."

Marge bit back irritation. Robert had needs, Caroline had needs, but she had needs of her own to deal with. Regardless of whether she had to share blame for Robert's problems, they had come at the wrong time for her to offer the support he seemed to expect. "Have you tried counseling?" she finally asked.

"No. Caroline suggested it, but I thought it was a waste of time. We should be able to talk this out and solve it like adults."

That didn't sound like Caroline always got her way. "I think you should reconsider. In the meantime, what will you do?"

"Can I move back here until I get squared away?" he asked. "I know she won't let me into the apartment tonight. I can stay here and help with expenses indefinitely while we all figure out what to do next."

For a moment, Marge felt a wave of relief wash over her. No more empty house. No more handling everything alone. No more worry about expenses.

She caught herself. Robert needed to work on his own future, something easy to neglect if he had the comforts of home. Caroline was right about that. And Marge didn't want to fall back into keeping house for Robert. She also needed to work on her future.

"No," Marge said, feeling guilty at first and then determined. "I'm sorry, Robert, but no. You can't afford to think of this house as a way station. It would be too easy to let time slip by without making other arrangements. Besides, we both need space to think about our next steps."

"I don't have enough money to move into a new apartment. Not right after the funeral expenses . . ." He stopped and clamped his mouth shut.

"I am going to repay you for the funeral expenses,"

Marge said. "That's what the ten thousand was for, and I'll give you a check for that before you leave. Anything over that I'll pay you after the BMW sells."

"Mother, this is all wrong," Robert cried. "You don't have to pay me back for anything. I have a good job and I can manage. In fact, I could support us both. Why won't you let me take care of you?"

"Because I don't need taking care of, Robert. I chose to let your father take care of me, but I'm finished with that part of my life. I want to be selfish. I want to live my own life. I want to think only about me for a while. If your marriage is truly finished, why don't you do the same?" Marge was amazed and a little disconcerted by her own words. She hadn't realized how strongly she felt them. It seemed almost like a betrayal of her life with Gene.

Robert sat staring bleakly at nothing for so long Marge wondered whether she should get up and leave him alone. When he spoke, his voice was barely above a whisper. "Because I'm scared," he said. "I'm not strong, like Dad was. I must have inherited Uncle Larry's genes. I'm afraid I can't make it on my own. That's probably what attracted me to Caroline. She's so strong and determined. But her job is more important to her than I am. I'm afraid that if she becomes too successful she won't want to stay with me. If we had children, she wouldn't leave. She might even want to quit working and stay home with them, like you did."

It was a few moments before Marge could find her voice. "You are more like your father than you know," she said. Although it had been a long time since she had allowed herself to admit this, she knew it was true. Gene had depended on her in many of the same ways Robert wanted to depend on Caroline. It made him able to look strong to the world . . . to his own son. The difference was that Marge had molded her life to fit that need for Gene, while Caroline insisted that she had a right to a life of her own.

The realization startled Marge. If that was true, then maybe it wasn't true Marge hadn't had the perseverance to make something out of her talent. Maybe she had stopped pursuing her art because it took time away from being the wife and mother she thought she was supposed to be.

"And wanted to be," Gene's voice whispered. "It wasn't all my fault."

Tears threatened. She had never admitted that either, but she realized the resentment had always been there. It grew when Gene seemed to turn away from her in the last few months. That was what had sent her looking for consolation from someone else. If only we were more honest with each other, she thought.

She shook her head and looked at Robert. "You might as well spend the night, but you have to make other arrangements tomorrow. I'll make out a check for the ten thousand from the insurance. When you get a chance, bring me a copy of the bills for actual expenses so I can pay you the rest." She went to the desk in the office to write out the check.

"The funeral expenses were less than ten thousand dollars," Robert said. "If you insist on paying them, they came to seven thousand eight hundred."

Marge wrote a check for that amount and helped Robert get his room ready for the night. Leaving him alone to call Caroline, to make sure she didn't send his belongings to the house, Marge took a glass of wine upstairs to her bedroom.

She left her clothes lay where they fell when she took them off, slipped into one of Gene's old shirts, and sat by the window in the chaise lounge that had been her fantasy purchase for the bedroom. She sipped her wine and gazed at the clouds flitting across the moon. Another day gone and she hadn't even begun to find out what happened to Gene. Perhaps she was being selfish, sending Robert away, but she needed to be by herself right now. Robert would have to solve his own problems.

"I always thought you could handle anything." Gene's voice broke her reverie.

Not fair. Not fair. "I let you do it all. I didn't try to control our lives," Marge responded.

"Maybe you should have."

"Would you have listened? You decided to go into business with Bruce, even though you knew I didn't want it. Did he hold a gun to your head? And what did you do in the last two months? Where did you put the money? Why did someone kill you? To keep you from getting it back?"

There were no answers and Marge closed her eyes in discouragement, letting tears flow unchecked.

Why wouldn't Bruce let the police see the check, she wondered just before falling asleep.

Marge opened her eyes to the soft swish of a steady, light rain. Disoriented, she turned her head and realized she was still on the chaise lounge, the almost full glass of wine on the table beside her. She sat up to see the alarm clock at the bedside—seven-thirty already. Pulling on her robe, she hurried downstairs in time to see Robert walking towards a waiting taxi, his coat pulled halfway over his head.

Marge padded on bare feet into the kitchen, switched on the percolator, and returned upstairs to shower and dress. As she sat at the table, savoring her first cup of coffee, she realized that, except for the slice of toast yesterday, she hadn't eaten breakfast all month. That was a twenty-seven-year-old habit she had broken pretty easily. She wasn't sure she had ever told Gene she didn't like food first thing in the morning. She had let him take it for granted they would breakfast together.

How many things had Gene never told her? She didn't think there could be many. She thought she was too attuned to his moods for him to keep secrets from her, yet he had kept his every movement secret from her for two months. There must be some clue as to where he had been or what he'd done.

The ad for selling the BMW wouldn't appear in the paper until Sunday. That gave her today and Saturday to finish other errands and to work on finding some answers.

Marge turned up the volume on the radio to chase away the silence and went to the office. She made a more thorough search through the desk drawers, this time looking for anything out of the ordinary. Nothing.

Of course, if Gene wanted to hide something from her, the unlockable desk in the middle of what should have been the dining room would not be a very good place to put it. Pouring another cup of coffee, she went upstairs and folded back Gene's closet doors.

She stood in front of them, immobilized. "I can't do this," she whispered.

She reached out, lifted the sleeve of Gene's best silk sports coat, and held it to her cheek. The last time Gene wore it was about a month before he died, at a party thrown by one of his customers who lived high up in Newport Hills, with an expansive view across Lake Washington to Seattle. She still carried the image of Gene that night; she remembered because she had noted how thin he had become while she wasn't paying attention. He leaned against the balcony railing and stared into the distance, toward the lights of Seattle twinkling on the night horizon across the lake. The blankness of his gaze gave Marge a sudden urge to reach out and touch him. She wanted to know what was going on beneath that distracted surface and what was happening to their well-ordered life. But their host had come out to hand Gene a fresh drink, and the moment passed.

She closed the closet door and leaned against it, shutting her eyes against the pain that tightened her chest. It would be nice to wait for some future day when she felt strong enough to handle Gene's clothes, but she couldn't. They might contain clues to what happened to him. Taking a deep breath, she re-opened the closet doors.

One at a time, she pulled suits, sports coats, slacks, and dress shirts from hangars. Eyes blurred with unshed tears; she searched every pocket before folding the clothes and packing them in boxes from the garage. Each time she closed a box, desolation swept through her. Another piece of Gene gone. Still, as long as she had to touch them, it only made sense to pack them up. That way she would only have to endure this pain once.

Gene was not extravagant, but she had filled several boxes with clothes plus a couple bags with shoes by the time she finished. The closet was empty of all but two worn shirts, gifts she had given Gene long ago that had remained favorites of his to wear around the house.

Even with the luggage carrier, it took three trips to bump the boxes down the stairs and into the garage to put them in the Honda. When the car was filled to capacity Marge sagged against the kitchen door. She had found nothing, and it was barely past eleven o'clock. The radio was no longer filling the emptiness in the house, which was beginning to close in on her. She had to get out for a while.

The rain had dwindled to a sporadic drizzle, still too much for the long walk that normally unwound her tensions. On impulse, she phoned Gene's younger brother, Larry, to confirm that he would be home, and discovered his phone had been disconnected. That worried her. Larry had been sober and holding down a job before Gene died. She drove to a Goodwill drop location, unloaded the car, and headed for I-90 East.

Larry was a born patsy. He could be talked into almost anything—and usually was. Later, he always had to be bailed out. It was usually Gene who did the bailing. In addition, the alcohol problem he developed prevented Larry from keeping whatever jobs he could find.

Marge tried, as she exited I-90 in Issaquah and wound through the woodsy May Valley Road to Larry's house, to imagine what Larry might have gotten himself into that would cause Gene to cash out all the money he could get his hands on. She shook her head. Gene wouldn't have done that for Larry, no matter how desperate his brother was. Gene did what he could to help Larry, but had declared years ago that his own family came first. Otherwise he would be condemning them to the same condition under which Larry's family had lived until his wife left him with their three children.

As Marge turned in at the driveway, she soaked in the awakening beauty of the woodsy setting. The only eyesore was the small rundown cottage from which Larry emerged. He looked terrible. His bloodshot eyes and scrubby three-day beard did not give him the appearance of recently coming into money.

Marge marveled, as she always had, at the lingering tenderness that had caused Larry's wife, Tammy, to refuse to sell the house while it was still livable to get her share out. Instead, she had worked some deal to put it in their children's names, giving Larry tenancy for as long as he lived.

No matter how much Larry goofed up, he would always have a home.

Of course, Tammy had never stopped working, so she was able to establish a life for herself and the children—one with more financial security than when she was married to Larry. Marge wondered where Tammy was and what she was doing. She could probably teach Marge a thing or two about self-sufficiency. Unfortunately, Tammy had cut off all connection with Larry's family after the divorce.

After Tammy and the kids left, Larry started drinking heavily and didn't hold a steady job for several years; not until Gene, after months of prodding, convinced him to go to AA. He had been sober for the last year and working for six months. It appeared Gene's death had driven him back to the bottle.

Tears stood in Larry's rheumy eyes as Marge submitted to a quick hug before pulling away. She wondered if Larry only bathed when he shaved.

"Come in, come in," Larry said, pulling at her arm. "It's good to see you out and about. You'll have to excuse the mess. Just haven't been myself since . . . you know."

Marge's throat constricted painfully as Larry turned his head away. Something in the movement, the fragility of the head and neck, was so like Gene in the last weeks. When Larry turned back the likeness disappeared in the roughness of his unkempt face.

Marge bumped into Larry when he stopped short in the doorway of the house. "Uh, on second thought, maybe I should bring some chairs outside," he said.

Marge peered around him. Every surface was covered with littered paper, clothing, and dirty dishes. Could this have happened in a month? She walked gingerly around Larry into the living room and peeked into the kitchen. A gaping hole in the cabinets announced the dishwasher was gone.

Marge's first impulse was to go back outside and let Larry bring the chairs. But, if she did that, she wouldn't be able to look inside for any evidence of what happened to Gene or the money. Taking a deep breath, she turned back to Larry.

"Don't be silly," she said. "In here will be fine."

"I didn't realize how bad it was," Larry muttered with such a hangdog look Marge had to stifle an urge to scratch behind his ears. Instead, she started gathering up clothing. "No, don't bother about that stuff," Larry objected. "I'll get to it sooner or later."

"I have to stay busy," Marge said with a forced smile. "Otherwise I get too emotional." She went to the closet and was surprised to find a clean pair of slacks and a shirt. Kept for emergencies? She pulled them out and ordered Larry into the bathroom. "Why don't you take a shower and change, then we'll run a load of laundry?" she said.

Larry started to argue, but gave in when Marge pushed him toward the bathroom. When Marge had a load of clothes ready to wash, she discovered the washer and dryer had also been removed.

Undaunted, Marge found a bag for the clothes and another for the trash scattered around the house. Double-checking every piece of paper before throwing it in the trash bag turned up nothing even remotely connected to Gene or the money.

Larry took a long time in the bathroom. By the time he finally emerged, having made an attempt at shaving, too, the living room was uncluttered and the last two eggs softened the one dry slice of bread she had found. She scrubbed caked on dishes while watching to make sure Larry ate every bite. By the time he finished eating his eyes had cleared slightly.

"Larry, why did Gene remove you as executor of his will?" Marge asked, pouring them each a cup of coffee and sitting where she could watch his face.

He peered across the table at her. "Did he? I had forgotten he ever asked me to do that."

"About five months before he died. Can you think of anything that happened around then that would explain why he did it?"

Larry was shaking his head, frowning with thought. "Do I look like someone you'd leave as executor of your will?" he asked, shrugging. "I'm surprised it took him that long. Maybe he finally realized that I'd never be anything but a disaster."

That was probably true. Larry's inability to handle the task was the reason Marge had never questioned Gene's decision to switch to his lawyer. Although the doctor told Gene he was going to die only two months before he was killed, Gene probably suspected the truth long before and had begun to look over his arrangements.

"Let's see, that would be some time late last year, wouldn't it?" Larry continued, still shaking his head. "He came out to see me, did you know that?"

Marge looked up. Tears filled his eyes again. She hadn't known. "Wanted to see his old brother before the end, I guess. Spent the whole day with me a few times. Did some fixing up and helped me clean out the place. Didn't do much the last couple of times he was here, though. He was kind of down. Told me I wasn't the only fool in the family."

"Did he say anything else about that?" Marge asked, holding her breath. "Anything about what he had done to make him feel that way?"

Marge wanted to grab Larry's still shaking head and hold it still. "No, not really. Something about how you couldn't trust anybody. How . . ." he paused, as if trying to remember the exact words. "How the most innocent-seeming people could be the most crooked. He said he finally understood how I got taken in sometimes. And . . ." Larry suddenly stopped shaking his head and smiled his old, direct smile. The one that kept people coming back to help him time and again, even after he had proven he was a lost cause. "And, he said that without you he would be in the same boat I was. He said you were what made his life work." Larry frowned. "He seemed sad when he said that. 'She doesn't deserve this,' he said."

"Did he ever mention a Cheltington Investment Company?"

"No, he never talked about money or business with me."

"Do you remember when his last visit was?" Marge asked.

The furrow in Larry's forehead deepened. "It wasn't long . . . about a week before he died, I think," he said.

Marge ducked her head to hide a sudden surge of tears. When she could steady her voice again, she asked, "Did Gene ever leave anything here with you? Or put anything down and forget to take it?"

Larry started to shake his head but then stopped. "Wait. He did leave a telephone. He said he wanted to be sure he could get in touch with me, so he bought a phone and paid for the phone service."

"Did he ever make calls from it himself?" she asked.

"Not that I know of," Larry said. "I had started working. Once in a while he'd be in the house when I got home, so I don't know what he might have been doing. He did call me once or twice, when he'd said he was coming over but then had to change his plans and couldn't make it. "

Marge continued to ask questions while she gathered up the rest of the dirty clothes and drove Larry to the Laundromat. While the clothes were in the machine, she took him to the grocery store and loaded up on frozen, boxed, and canned meals. As she paid for them, she wondered how long it would be before she needed help buying groceries for herself.

That seemed to be the extent of Larry's knowledge about Gene's last months. It appeared Gene had spent quite a few days with Larry, but Larry's memory was fuzzy enough to make it hard to learn specifics. What Larry remembered wasn't enough to account for two full months, but if Gene had spent several days in a variety of different places, that might explain how he kept up the pretense of going to work. At least what Larry said showed Gene hadn't been spending all of his time with someone else.

By the time she and Larry returned to his half-clean house with his freshly done laundry and a week's worth of groceries, Marge knew she could never seriously suspect Larry of having anything to do with the money or Gene's death. She also knew there was no real information to gain from him. She was tempted to leave, since any improvement she made in Larry's house would probably be short-lived, but the remotest possibility that Gene had left something else in the house made her decide to complete the cleaning job.

All she found, wadded up beside the wood stove as if it had fallen out when the door was opened, was a report confirming the terminal nature of Gene's illness. It gave him equally undesirable options: undergoing treatment that would lengthen his life by a matter of weeks, or at best months, but make it miserable; or not undergoing treatment and dying sooner.

Marge assumed he had chosen the latter. Otherwise he would have had to talk with her about the effects of the treatment. He must have come straight to Larry's after getting the report.

Marge sat on the floor and cried, wetting the paper as she smoothed it on her knee. Why hadn't he come to her? Larry stood over her, awkwardly rubbing her shoulder.

"Did Gene ever tell you he was sick?" Marge asked. She didn't know if she wanted to hear that he had shared the burden with someone other than herself.

"No," Larry said. "I had no idea." That didn't make Marge feel any better. She couldn't bear the thought of Gene living alone with the terrible knowledge, either.

But he had told Bruce.

"Larry, please get yourself back to AA," Marge said when his house was spotless and searched, with no further results.

"I will," he promised. Marge saw a resolve in his eyes that allowed her to hope it would happen. "I'm going next door to call as soon as you leave."

She kissed him gently on the cheek before getting into the Honda for the return to Bellevue. She hoped she wouldn't lose touch with Gene's only brother, but she couldn't help him. Her life was complicated enough.

The most innocent-seeming people could be the most crooked. Marge pondered Larry's words as she wended her way back to the expressway. Charles and Bruce both appeared to be innocent in this case. Was one of them the most crooked?

CHAPTER 5

GENE WAS KILLED in his own home. Could Bruce or Charles have come and gone without Marge knowing about it? She remembered one of the reasons the police gave for writing Gene's death off as a suicide was the lack of evidence that any force was used, either against Gene or to get into the garage. And, of course, Gene's keys were in the ignition. Would Gene have given house keys to either Bruce or Charles? She couldn't imagine why.

Marge was still mulling it over when she pulled into the driveway, barely noticing that the sun had finally pushed away the lingering clouds. Her brain befuddled with questions, she stumbled into the house. The door was no sooner closed than she heard a tentative knock.

Marge opened the door to Lori Knowles, who had been her best friend in the neighborhood. T-ball, Cub Scouts, baseball, and football; Lori and Marge had both been involved in these kids' activities up to their elbows. The difference was, Lori also held a full-time job. Marge always believed that was why Lori had remained so slender.

Today Lori's thick, almost black hair was stylish in a French plait that ran down the back of her neck. Her equally dark brown eyes, always calm and focused, were framed by the thickest lashes Marge had ever seen. Lori was the last person Marge expected to abandon her in her time of need.

Lori pushed a dish of her famous asparagus chicken salad into the doorway, as if she were afraid Marge would close the door on her. "I noticed how busy you've been for the last couple of days and thought it might be nice to have something different for dinner," she said with a significant glance at the Watson's house.

Marge looked away from Lori to disguise the tears that threatened. She caught Wilma staring out the window next door and remembered her bitter words about people who never showed up after the first two weeks.

"I hope you can forgive me," Lori went on, as if reading Marge's thoughts. "I hurt so much for you, I didn't know what to do or say. So, like an idiot, I ended up doing nothing. I wish I had been a better friend when you needed one."

The silence stretched until it became uncomfortable. "Come in," Marge finally said. "Join me for some iced tea?"

Marge's hands shook so hard she nearly slopped the iced tea she poured into two glasses. Why had she invited Lori in? She could understand her other neighbors' reluctance to visit in the last month. What could they say to someone whose spouse was believed to have committed suicide? How could they include a widow in their lives that are filled with couples? But, Lori . . . Lori was her closest friend and confidante, the person she would have thought would always be there for her.

As if sensing Marge's thoughts again, Lori shrugged her shoulders, which Marge knew indicated more discomfort than Lori was ever able to openly show. "I know I neglected you, and I'm truly sorry," she said. "It was so difficult to come, that I convinced myself this was one of those times when solitude is the best thing. I was reluctant to disturb you until you were ready. The only problem was, I couldn't figure out when that would be."

Marge knew she wanted back the friendship she and Lori had shared. If they could pick up where they had left off, would forgiveness come in time? The only way to find out was to try. She started by talking about what she had learned in the last two days and didn't stop until Lori was up-to-date.

Lori didn't waste time commiserating. Without a word, she went to the phone and called her older son, Brian, who was taking a long weekend break from his University of Washington studies. "Get a couple of the neighborhood kids and gather up car washing gear. You've got a job over here at Marge's."

"Oh, no, that's not necessary . . ." Marge began, but Lori didn't give her time to finish.

"Kids sometimes have better instincts than their parents. All of them kept coming to our house and asking what they could do to help you, but we didn't have an answer for them. This seems like as good a way as any."

Brian soon arrived with several younger kids and directed the action. With buckets and rags and the garden hose, they went to work scrubbing and buffing, then hooked up a vacuum and cleaned the inside just as thoroughly. Once finished with the BMW, they repeated the process with the Honda. Even then, they didn't stop. When both cars were spotless they tackled the winter's residue of leaves and debris and trimmed the edges of the lawn.

When they couldn't find anything else to do, Brian came to the door. "We'll mow the lawn when it has had a chance to dry out a little," he said.

"What good work you do!" Marge exclaimed, looking over his shoulder. All the other kids had left quietly and quickly. "I'll have to find some way to thank all of you."

Brian laughed. "Why do you think they all left so fast?" he asked. "They don't want to be embarrassed by thanks for something they wanted to do. I only stopped to give you this paper we found in the glove compartment, in case it means something. Oh, and you should find something to deodorize the inside of the BMW. I don't think our cleaning did the trick."

"Thank you, I'll look into that. Remind me to ask Wilma to bake a plate of gingerbread cookies for you all," she said, taking the slip of paper. As Brian walked away, Marge sensed motion at the Watson's front window. A moment later their door opened and Willy stood in its frame.

"I'm glad to see you two together again . . . finally," he said. His voice didn't sound happy. It sounded cold, almost angry.

Marge realized Willy might have a harder time accepting Lori's apology than she did. "Good friends are too hard to come by to lose any," was all she could think of to say.

"Good, good," Willy said halfheartedly before backing through his door and closing it.

"Can you forgive me, Marge?"

Marge turned to face Lori.

"I know it is easy to say this and not mean it, but I truly do mean it. I don't want to lose you as a friend because of what happened. I know I should have found some way to comfort you during this last month. Obviously Willy knows it, too. I'm so sorry."

Marge found herself enveloped in Lori's arms. After a moment's hesitation she returned the hug. Her voice was muffled in Lori's shoulder. "I can't imagine not having you for a friend. If you think you need to be forgiven, then you are."

"Thank you. Good luck with the car on Sunday. I have to get going so I can finish preparing dinner for my ravenous crew; but I promise, I won't be a stranger any more."

After Lori left, Marge looked at the slip of paper Brian had given her. It contained an address and a phone number. Stumbling to the phone, Marge dialed with shaky fingers.

"Barrington's Executive Search," a smooth voice said.

Marge swallowed hard. "May I speak to the manager, please?" she asked, wondering if executive search firms had managers.

"I'll see if Mr. Barrington is still here," the voice purred.

Marge glanced at her watch. It was nearly five o'clock. She held her breath until a man's voice came on the line.

"This is Henry Barrington. What can I do for you?"

"My name is Marge Christensen. My husband, Gene, died recently. I found your number among his personal possessions and wondered if he contacted you."

"Yes, Mrs. Christensen, I remember your husband. A highly qualified man. I felt I would have no trouble placing him in a good position. I had set up two interviews for him, even though he was reluctant to move quite so fast; but, of course, he wasn't able to appear at either of them. Please accept my sympathy for your loss."

"Did Gene tell you why he was looking for a position?" Marge asked.

"He said he'd been in a business of his own, but found the demands of running it left him with too little time for his family. He wished to lighten up his responsibilities in order to spend more time with you."

That certainly sounded like what she wanted, but why would Gene look for a job if he knew he was ill and possibly dying?

"I'm a little confused, because I didn't know my husband was looking for a job," she said. "Did he indicate when he would be available for work?"

"It's interesting you should ask that. He told me he wouldn't be able to make any definite commitment for at least a week. I got the feeling he was waiting to see if he got some other job offer before getting too far along with interviews through my firm."

Or waiting to see if the doctor said he would live long enough to accept a job, Marge thought as she hung up.

The doorbell rang. Marge sighed and dashed the tears that had been about to spill over. She wished for some of the solitude Lori had thought she needed as she opened the door to Willy and Wilma.

"We wanted to make sure you were all right," Willy said.

"And to find out what excuse Lori had for the shamefaced way she has behaved this last month," Wilma added.

"Now, Wilma," Willy said, a chuckle in his voice. "That's none of our business."

Marge had to laugh. Willy's sharp eyes told Marge he was as curious as Wilma was, even if he was reluctant to admit it.

"Lori apologized for not knowing how to behave," she said. "And she got the kids to do all that work for me. Don't you think that should count for something?"

"She didn't load you down with any problems of her

own, I hope," Wilma chattered. "You have enough to deal with as it is."

"Problems? No. Is she having problems?" Marge asked, her brow wrinkling.

"Wilma is just being a mother hen again," Willy said, "protecting you when you don't need protecting. Pay no attention to her. I see Lori brought you something for your dinner."

"Have you even had lunch?" Wilma asked. "You've been gone most of the day. You must remember to keep up your strength."

Marge laughed again. "Yes, mother hen, I will be sure to do that. You get a break from providing my food today. But, I do have a favor to ask. The ad for selling the BMW will be in Sunday's paper. When people start coming over to look at it, could you keep an eye out the window, to make sure everything's on the up and up? There are a lot of kooks out there these days."

"Of course we will," Willy promised. "And I'll have a baseball bat right by the door in case I have to chase anyone off."

Marge was sure he would. When they had finally gone, Marge realized she had, indeed, forgotten to eat lunch. It would be an early dinner as she suddenly felt starved. Saving Lori's salad for tomorrow, she grabbed containers of leftover cashew chicken and rice out of the refrigerator, poured them in a bowl, and stuck the bowl in the microwave. The Chinese food reminded her that Robert might not have a place to stay tonight.

She phoned the apartment he and Caroline shared, but there was no answer. Probably neither was home from work yet. She tried his office number, in case he was working late, but there was no answer there either. She hoped he had found somewhere to stay. She felt a wave of guilt at her edict he could only stay one night. She hoped he hadn't taken it too literally. She had just wanted to make sure he didn't camp here indefinitely.

Marge pulled the food out of the microwave and, while she ate it, called Kate at the apartment she shared with two other graduate students.

"Hi, Mom. How's it going?" Kate asked, sounding more like her old, bright self than she had in a long time.

"Busy," Marge answered. "I'm hardly in the house anymore. Someday I have to face things, like dusting. Kate, have you heard from Robert?"

"No. Why? Isn't he home?"

"Unless he patched things up with Caroline, they split up yesterday. Robert stayed here last night, but I told him he couldn't do it again and I can't get in touch with him to find out if he has a place to stay. Has he called you?"

"No, not yet." Kate didn't sound surprised. "But, don't worry, he will if nothing else works out. And, he can crash on our couch for a night or two if he needs to. What happened?"

Marge took a deep breath. "He had some idea about moving back here with Caroline and having children and I could keep house and tend to the children because Caroline doesn't want to quit working. Since he hadn't talked it over with Caroline beforehand, she was understandably furious. In her tirade she made it quite clear how little she thinks of me and my child-raising methods."

"Boy," Kate said with a little explosion of breath, "he really did it this time. But they have had fights before, and they always get back together . . ."

"Have they?" Marge was startled. "I didn't know that."

"Oh, yes," Kate said. "Robert has slept on my couch several times in the past few months. It's good you kicked him out, though. He might find it easier to let things slide if he had all the comforts of home around him."

"Including Mama to wait on him?"

Kate laughed. "Yes, I can see Caroline was angry. But, Mom, it's not your fault. Robert is who he is, and that's the person Caroline married. If she wanted someone different, she shouldn't have married him. He has never pretended about how he feels or thinks."

"Well, thanks for the encouraging words. Oh, have you heard from your friend about business license applications?"

"Yes, and everything seems to be okay. He found no new applications in either Dad or Bruce's names. He did find the record of a change in the partnership, two weeks after Dad died. Does that sound right?"

"Two weeks *after*? Bruce told me he had to find the new partner before he could buy Gene out, and that the new partner had been in the office for weeks."

"Hmmm. Maybe they didn't complete the paperwork until after the new partner started working. Or it could take some time to get these things registered. I'll see if I can find out what exactly what the change was and how the date applies," Kate said. "I saw Dad's lawyer, by the way."

"Really? Where?" Marge didn't know why she was so surprised. Charles must have some kind of life of his own.

"A group of us went for a drink on Broadway, after class yesterday. As we were leaving, I saw Mr. Froyell going into a restaurant with a woman. His wife maybe?"

Marge swallowed hard before answering. "He's not married. Must have been a client or a date," she said, tripping over the last word. "What did she look like?"

"She was a mousy little thing. Looked kind of sad," Kate said. "Not at all the type I'd think he would date."

Marge stared at the phone after hanging up. *A mousy little thing. Kind of sad.* Did that sound like the Marge of a few weeks ago? If Charles involved with another woman, then what was his word worth?

She shook her head. Even if he was seeing another woman, that didn't make him a killer. Anyway, the woman could just as easily be a client in the middle of a divorce.

At least the news answered one question for her. Except for a slight dent in her pride, she discovered she didn't care at all if Charles was involved with someone else.

CHAPTER 6

~

T HE CLOTHES IN GENE'S dresser had fewer pockets, making the search of them go fast on Saturday morning. Marge saved a few sweatshirts and sweaters, and packed or trashed the rest. She didn't expect to find anything in the clothes drawers, and she didn't.

She saved his odds and ends drawer for last—but before tackling it, she got a refill of coffee.

Her hands moved slower and slower as she rediscovered the small pictures, tokens, and mementos of work achievements and family pleasures Gene had accumulated over the years. They stopped altogether when she found the family picture he always had on his desk at the office. It was the last family portrait they had taken, when Robert was about ten and Kate eight. Why hadn't they taken other family photos as the children grew? I guess we always thought there would be time for it tomorrow. Then the children were grown. And time ran out.

She placed the photo on top of the dresser and forced herself to go back to work. Mixed in with the memorabilia were several odd-sized slips of paper, evidently whatever had been close at hand when needed, on which were jotted telephone numbers and bits of information.

Putting the items she wanted to keep in her own drawer and things for the kids back into Gene's drawer, Marge went downstairs and tossed the trash. After putting the Goodwill boxes in the Honda, she took the slips of paper to the desk. Maybe no one would answer on Saturday, but it was worth a shot.

The first two calls turned out to be easy. They were businesses Gene would have been involved with in his line of work, and a recording announced the weekday business hours during which they were open.

Two other numbers were executive employment agencies. "Gene, Gene," she sighed, closing her eyes. "How long were you going to wait before you told me?" She would phone them on Monday to see if she could find out anything new.

The answering machine response to another number indicated it was an investment firm with which they had never done business; at least Marge didn't think they had. Who knew what Gene had done in the last month? She hit redial. She had heard right. The name on the answering machine wasn't Cheltington Investment Company; it was Dorsey and Company. Could Gene have used a different firm to invest the money from the business? She would phone both companies on Monday.

When Marge checked the telephone book, she could not find a listing for Cheltington Investment Company. A call to directory assistance confirmed there was no such company listed in the metropolitan Seattle area. Perhaps the company wasn't in the Seattle area. But why would Gene use an investment firm outside the city?

The phone rang.

"Hello, Mother? This is Robert. I wanted to let you know that Caroline and I are back together."

"I'm glad, Robert," Marge said. Was she?

"Uh . . . you might be happy to hear we are going to start marriage counseling." He sounded more dispirited than Marge thought he ought to, right after making up with his wife; but that was understandable considering what agreeing to marriage counseling must have done to his pride. "Uh . . . I don't think I'll be able to see you for a week or two. Caroline is still pretty sore, and it'll take some time for her to cool off."

Caroline was sore? Marge felt her jaw clench. What about all those things Caroline had said about her?

"I understand, dear," she finally managed. "Right now, your most important job is to rebuild your marriage."

"And, uh, I ought to let you know that we're going to look for a condominium north of Lake Washington, probably in Seattle. Caroline says she can't continue to commute over the bridge. And, since I work in Bellevue, we'll find some place in between. I don't like moving farther away from you, but . . ."

Marge's laughter burst out, releasing her tension. "North of the lake is hardly an insurmountable distance, Robert," she said. To change the subject, she quickly asked, "Were you able to find anything about the Cheltington Investment Company?"

"No, I can't find any reference to it anywhere. I'll keep looking, though. By the way, I noticed the pencil drawer in the desk in my room is stuck. I'm sorry I didn't fix it the other night; I'll try to get over some time and do it."

Marge blinked, frowned, then shook her head. Maybe she hadn't given Robert all his strange ideas after all. She had never relied on Gene to fix much around the house. "I think I can manage to unstick it myself, but thanks for the offer."

Hanging up, Marge sank back in the chair and closed her eyes. After a minute she took a deep breath, sat up, and took out the check and savings books. She had a couple thousand dollars to hold her until the BMW sold. And that should be enough until she recovered their money.

What if she didn't recover the money? How long would, at most, twenty-two thousand dollars last? She wished she had encouraged Gene to keep his term life insurance another six years—at least until the mortgage was paid off. She couldn't have predicted their savings would disappear, but since she didn't work, the term insurance would have eased her financial situation even if they hadn't.

Robert and Caroline were buying their own place. Kate would have her apartment and a busy life. Since they were both settling nearby, Marge didn't need space for them to come home to. Even her own bedroom seemed less like home, now that she had removed Gene's things.

The roof needed to be looked at before next winter. Thank God they had the house painted last summer, although it would need to be done again in a few years. She had been waiting until both children completed their education before remodeling the kitchen. It was clean and in good working order, but it could definitely use some upgrading. That wouldn't get done now.

If she had to get a job, would she be able to keep up with the yard work as well as the housework? She wouldn't be able to afford help with the heavy outside work anymore.

Marge wandered into the eating area. She heard the children's footsteps and felt Gene's presence. She sat in the rocking chair and rocked gently back and forth. She had raised her family in this house. It was filled with memories: Gene laughing and adding a smudge of paint to her face when they were converting Kate's room from an infant's to a little girl's dream room. Robert and Kate racing through the house, happily secure, as only children who have never been uprooted can be. Kate coming down the stairs dressed for her first prom; Robert shooting hoops in the driveway.

But, memories wouldn't feed her.

She had no marketable skills and no assets except the BMW and the house. The realization of where her thoughts were leading made Marge stop rocking and sit up straight.

If she sold the house and invested the money? Could she earn enough interest to pay for the rent of a small apartment?

She rocked for a while longer, trying to convince herself to wait, to not rush into anything. She stopped rocking again and nodded in decision. She would investigate the idea of selling the house. She could always change her mind.

Despite her bravery, Marge felt a little like Alice falling down the rabbit hole. So many changes, so fast.

Before fear could make her delay, she looked in the yellow pages and found the numbers for three of the best-known real estate agencies in western Washington. When she finished calling, she had three appointments scheduled for late that afternoon. She sat by the phone for a few minutes, her head spinning.

"Why don't you tell me to slow down?" she whispered. "Or warn me that I'm going too fast, like you always did?"

She no longer had someone telling her when to stop. No one to warn her to think things through. She would have to be her own brakes.

After another trip to Goodwill to empty the Honda,

Marge returned and spent the rest of the morning cleaning. She was sure Realtors had seen worse, but as long as she had the house, she felt like a housewife, and a good housewife kept a clean house, as she had done for the last twenty-four years.

She grinned. That in itself was a good reason to sell the house.

After devouring a heaping plate of Lori's asparagus chicken salad for lunch, Marge took Gene's phone system from the closet. After a couple of false starts, she managed to get it hooked up and record her message on the answering machine. She phoned Lori and asked her to call back to make sure it worked. It did. Two minutes later Lori was ringing the doorbell.

"I thought you had voice mail," Lori said, as she watched Marge tinker with the machine.

"I do, but that costs money. I'm canceling it Monday. I can do everything I need to do on this machine." Marge set it to activate after four rings so that, until she got it cancelled, the machine would catch the calls before they went into voice mail.

"I know there is a way to store messages on this thing," Marge added. Pushing a button, she was startled to hear a robotic voice state a date and time, and then a woman's voice come on. Marge stopped the machine with shaking hands, took a deep breath, and pressed the button to begin again.

The date was more than three months ago. "Mr. Christensen, this is Colleen from Dr. Marrow's office, confirming your appointment for this coming Tuesday," the woman's voice said. Lori put a comforting arm around Marge's shoulders as they listened. The next three messages were also from Colleen, verifying appointments.

"These doctor appointments account for another chunk of his time," Marge whispered.

"You know he wasn't seeing another woman, Marge; no matter what anyone else says," Lori said. "Gene wouldn't do that to you."

"I think I know that," Marge answered. "But I'm only beginning to account for how Gene spent the last month of his life."

A man's voice—loud, forceful, and vaguely familiar—startled them. He didn't give a name. "Gene, I just found out the partnership is going to close to new investors next month. If you want to get on board, you need to do it, immediately." The message ended as abruptly as it had begun.

Marge stopped the machine, stared at Lori, and hit Replay Message. They listened to it three more times.

"I know that voice," Marge said. "I know I've heard it before. But I can't place it."

"It sounds familiar to me, too," Lori said. "Either we both know the person speaking or his voice is similar to that of someone we know."

Marge shook her head and ran the tape again. She tried to connect the voice with Charles or Bruce, but it didn't sound right. Besides, why would Bruce leave a message on the answering machine when he could talk to Gene in the office? She could only be sure it wasn't Larry. His voice would never be that firm again.

"Do you suppose he's speaking that way to disguise his voice?" Marge asked. "The only person I ever heard speak that firmly was my father and, when he did, we knew we'd better listen or else."

"It sounds like Gene wasn't sure about making that investment," Lori said. "This guy must have pressured him into it."

Marge nodded. "That might explain why he went ahead, but since he knew he might be dying, he still needed to be convinced it was sound enough to take care of me. 'The most innocent-seeming people turn out to be the most crooked,' he told his brother. It had to be someone he trusted completely."

"Do you have any idea who it could be?"

Marge shook her head. "I can only think of a couple people that fill the bill, but this voice doesn't sound like either of them."

"Are you going to give the tape to the police?"

Marge thought about it. "Eventually. But first I want to try it out on a few people and see if we can identify the speaker. It will be useless to the police unless we do."

"Frank told me he saw Gene's partner the other night."

"Bruce Wilcox? Where was that?"

"Frank took a client to that new casino the Mukleshoot Indians opened. He said Bruce was looking pretty serious about what was happening at the roulette wheel."

Marge had to laugh. "I never knew Bruce to look anything but serious—regardless of what he was doing. I think it's a look he has cultivated to impress clients."

A few minutes later, Lori went back home to help Frank pack for a business trip he was leaving on the next morning. "I don't know why he can't fly on company time," she said as she walked out the door.

After Lori left, Marge played the tape three more times. It took all her willpower not to throw the answering machine against the floor in frustration. The identity of the voice danced just outside her grasp. Try as she might, she couldn't connect it with Bruce, Charles, or anyone else.

The first Realtor arrived at three o'clock. After a quick look through the house he said, "How does four hundred thousand sound to you? Of course, we'd list it for three hundred ninety-nine thousand and negotiate from there."

Marge's jaw dropped. It sounded wonderful, of course. Also unbelievable. This wasn't one of those mansions up in Newport Hills with an expansive view. "Are they really selling that high?" she asked.

"Going up every day," the Realtor assured her. "The value is increased because of your Newport Hills address—even if you do sit down low."

As astonished as Marge was at the high price the first Realtor suggested, the second one equally deflated her.

"Two hundred and fifty thousand?" she asked.

"People know what happened here," the Realtor informed her. "That will make the house harder to sell. Still, you might get a better price if you aren't in a hurry and can do a little fixing up."

Marge swallowed hard. She hadn't thought about Gene's suicide affecting her ability to sell the house. "Fixing up? How?" she asked.

"Well, new paint. New cabinet surfaces. Maybe some updated flooring and window treatment."

"Wait a minute," Marge objected. "I'm selling the house because I need money. I can't afford all that."

By the time the third agent arrived, Marge was totally confused. She opened the door and stepped back, trying to cover her momentary surprise. She had expected to see the man with whom she had talked with on the phone. Instead, a woman who didn't look anything like a real estate agent smiled at her. She was tall and slender, with slightly mussed shoulder-length blonde hair and laugh lines crinkling the corners of startling blue eyes. She looked as if she would be more at home seeking nirvana in a commune than selling houses in suburbia.

"Hello. My name is Melissa Horton. Here is my card." She paused, seemed to sense Marge's confusion. "You spoke to my broker on the phone. He rarely does listing calls himself. He prefers to handle the administrative side of the business." With a wicked little grin, she added, "Actually, he's too busy enjoying the fruits of our labors on the golf course."

Marge laughed, immediately feeling comfortable. She showed Melissa around the house for the usual inspection, questions, and measuring, before leading her to the kitchen table, where Melissa spread out a sheaf of papers.

"I'd suggest you start at around three twenty. That's close to what the last three houses in similar neighborhoods sold for," she said, showing Marge color pictures and descriptions of the houses. "Your home is in better repair than the last house that sold, this one on the next block that went for two thirty-five. And yours has nice eye appeal, even though it could use a little updating."

"The roof is original, though I haven't had any problems with it."

"We'll know if we need to allow for that after the inspection."

"And, I do need to sell quickly."

Melissa glanced sharply at her. "The market has improved since that last house sold." She showed Marge sales statistics from the last three months compared to the same time a year ago to prove her point.

If Marge had been confused before, now she was totally lost. How could she make a decision this large without Gene here to guide her? She hedged. "How do I know which one is right?" she asked Melissa. "I didn't expect the quotes to be so far apart. And why shouldn't I go for the highest one—that's the one that sounds best to me?"

"I don't know how they came up with prices very far from this one," Melissa said. "Did the other agents show you the comparable sales they used to determine the asking price?"

Marge shook her head.

"Ask them to do that. Then, ask to see a record of their performance in the area." She pulled out another sheet and handed it to Marge. It contained a list of all the houses sold in the lower area of Factoria Square and the upper Newport Hills in the last year, what realty firm had listed it, which one sold it, and compared the asking price with the sales price. "Show them this, and ask them if we missed anything."

"What about . . ." Marge hesitated. "What about the fact that my husband died in the garage? How will that affect my ability to sell?"

"It may take a little longer to find a buyer who doesn't worry about that kind of thing," Melissa said. "And the buyer may bargain a little harder knowing the circumstances. But, we can cross that bridge during negotiations when it comes up."

"Does it have to come up?"

"I think so. It is best to be open about everything, so the buyer has no cause to come back to you later with complaints. You don't need that kind of complication."

"Everything you say makes sense. And I am impressed with all the information you've prepared for me," Marge said. She hesitated. "This is such a big step for me. I'm still not sure if it's the right thing to do."

"I understand perfectly," Melissa said, starting to gather up her papers. "Take all the time you need."

Marge almost grabbed Melissa's arm to prevent her from leaving. She didn't want to be alone in this quandary.

Waiting for divine intervention wasn't going to work: neither Gene nor God was going to make this decision for her. I can do it, she thought. It doesn't matter how long I wait, I don't belong in this house anymore.

Looking at Melissa and the preparation she had done for this meeting, Marge took a deep breath. "No, I don't want to delay it," she said.

Melissa didn't pressure Marge to sign the papers immediately. Instead, she coaxed Marge to talk about the house, her reasons for selling it, and her hesitation.

"I do wonder if I'm going too fast. Yet, I'm sure I can't afford to keep it. And I certainly don't need all this space. I still have six years to pay on the mortgage, and major repairs, like that roof, are bound to come up."

"Tell you what," Melissa said. "When an agent lists a house and a full price offer comes in, you are obligated to sell. But, no one gives a full price offer, and my broker gives us a lot of leeway. We can put it on the market. If an offer comes in and you decide you don't want to sell at that time, I can refuse the offer.

"My own feeling is that you should sell the house. Financially, even if you recover your other savings, it's the best thing to do. It is a family house and it doesn't make sense to continue upkeep on it when you're alone. The only question is whether you should wait until you've had time to adjust to your husband's death first—and only you can decide that."

Marge nodded. "I understand what you're saying, and I appreciate the lengths you're willing to go to help me. I agree I need to sell it and I don't think I can afford to wait for the psychologically correct time. Let's get it done."

After Marge had signed and initialed a seemingly endless

stream of papers, she sat back and sighed again. "What do we do next?"

"Tomorrow morning I'll put a For Sale sign up in the yard and take a photo for the Multiple Listing Service. I think next Sunday we should have an open house."

"And, when the house does sell, how long will it take to complete the settlement?"

"That depends on how long it takes to get the buyer's mortgage approved. I would guess six to eight weeks."

It was nearly six by the time they finished their business. Melissa filed the papers in her briefcase.

"Are you finished working for the day?" Marge asked, feeling the emptiness of the house close in again. "Would you like a glass of wine? Or some coffee? Or do you have a family you need to get home to?"

Melissa smiled. "No, no family. Yes, I'm finished for the day." She paused. "Yes, a glass of white wine would be nice."

Marge poured two glasses of Riesling and found a jar of dry roasted peanuts to offer with it.

"I didn't think to ask about probate. Are you sure you're legally entitled to sell the house?" Melissa asked.

"I'm sure I am," Marge said. "I'll ask my attorney, Charles Froyell, on Monday. Unless he tells me something different, let's go ahead as planned."

Melissa frowned. "Charles Froyell? Where have I heard that name before? I believe he's the attorney for another client of mine who was recently widowed and selling her house. She seemed a little taken with him."

Marge stared at her. "You don't happen to know if she lost any money, do you?"

"Not that she mentioned. She didn't seem to be in any financial trouble."

"You couldn't give me her name by any chance?" Marge asked.

Melissa hesitated. "I don't think I should do that without her permission. Why don't I contact her and see if she's willing to call you?"

"Fair enough. I appreciate your discretion. A refill on the wine?" Marge asked.

Melissa rose with a swan-like grace that seemed to be a part of her nature. "No, thank you. This was a lovely way to end the day, but I need to get going. I'll be by some time tomorrow to put up the For Sale sign and take some pictures.

As Melissa drove away, Marge closed the door and leaned against it, gazing around the house that soon might not be hers. She was surprised to feel herself starting to detach already. Still, she didn't want it to sell too fast. Not until she had solved the mystery of Gene's death and the disappearance of their money. When she started her new life, she wanted to leave the ghosts here . . . which meant she had better get a move on in solving the riddles.

For starters, she wondered how many lonely widows were sweet on Charles Froyell—and if any of them had found their life savings missing too.

CHAPTER 7

THE UNEXPECTED SUNLIGHT invited Marge to make an early start of her Sunday. Going to the nine o'clock service at church, rather than the later one, would allow her to be home before any calls came in about the BMW. Plus, she found the smaller, early service easier to handle while her emotions were so raw.

Despite the weather's invitation to indulge in bright colors, she stuck to a soft-brown knit dress. She wanted to dress in yellow for Gene, but the elderly members of the congregation might think it unseemly for a recent widow.

Marge had no sooner sat down to coffee and the newspaper than the phone rang. It was Charles.

"I thought the weekend might be a little lonely for you," he said. "Could I interest you in brunch? Perhaps at the end of a drive up to Snoqualmie Pass?"

His voice was soft; comforting. It wouldn't be surprising to learn several widows had fallen for him. But how would his voice sound when he tried to be forceful?

"Thank you, but no, Charles," she replied, trying to keep the chill she felt out of her voice. "I'm busy selling Gene's car today, so I'm just going to pop in at the early church service and come right back home. I don't have time to be lonely."

Which wasn't exactly true. Having things to do didn't eradicate the loneliness. It just created a layer of activity on top of it. And she did have to get together with Charles, but first she had to figure out her plan of attack.

"I'm glad to hear you are keeping busy." He sounded as if he were disappointed but trying hard to be gallant. Marge almost laughed. *What an actor.* "Perhaps we can get together sometime this week to handle your IRA rollover and any other loose ends."

"Yes, let's do that. I'll let you know when I have some time," Marge said.

The phone rang as soon as she hung up, chasing Charles from her mind.

"You put in the ad about the BMW?"

"Yes."

"How much do you want?"

"Twenty-two thousand."

"What? That's too much."

"Okay," Marge said. Shaking her head and grinning, she hung up the phone and set the answering machine to come on after the first ring. She'd deal with all the calls after she returned from church.

Her church family may have stopped visiting her, but they made sure Marge felt cared for and welcome when she attended the services. The first Sunday after Gene's death she felt so exposed when she was in church, but no one pointed. No one seemed to be whispering about suicide behind her back.

Today, like that first Sunday, she felt tension she hadn't realized was tying her in knots melt away in the outpouring of care and concern.

"Marge, Marge. It's so good to see you." Brent Larson, one of the most active church members, wrapped her in a big bear hug. "I can't tell you how often we think about you. And Gene. I don't know how we could have finished the painting without him."

Marge gave him a blank stare.

"Didn't he tell you? Gene was over here almost every day the month before he died. Every time you walk into a classroom, the parlor, or the dining hall, you can see his handiwork."

"Did he talk to anyone in particular while he worked?" Marge asked. "There is so much I don't know about the weeks before he died; it might help me find out what happened to him."

"We usually worked together," Brent said. "He was more serious than usual and often seemed lost in thought. Knowing now that he was ill makes his silence understandable. The last few days he seemed frazzled. I asked him if something was wrong, but he didn't want to talk about it. After Gene died and all the facts came out, I figured he had found out his illness was terminal."

"That was in the last week?" Marge asked, puzzled.

"Yes. I remember, because it was only that last week that Gene went off to eat lunch by himself rather that sit with the rest of us."

"He'd already known for a week or more that his illness was terminal," Marge said. She decided not to share the rest of her thoughts with Brent. Perhaps Gene found out about whatever the problem was with their life savings that final week.

"I did overhear his side of what appeared to be a heated telephone conversation the last day he was here," Brent said. "Come to think of it, it was the day before he died."

The gathering music began so Brent went to join his wife. "I'll see you after church," he promised.

Marge sat through the service, trying unsuccessfully to keep her mind on the pastor's words. Gene must have been desperate to keep his illness from her—even making sure she never saw or smelled any traces of the paint that would have required an explanation for why he wasn't at work. She realized that a lot of Gene's time after he sold his share of the business was being accounted for, little by little. As suspicious as his activities seemed, she had never been able to convince herself he was seeing someone else. Marge felt she was close to being able to prove at least that much to the police. Along with her prayers, she sent a silent plea to Gene to forgive her for her doubts and for her own wandering attentions.

The slow line moving out of the church was usually a pleasure. Marge enjoyed talking with other members and looked forward to greeting the pastor, who gave undivided attention to each person who filed past. Today, though, seeing Brent leave the sanctuary far ahead of her tempted Marge to slip out a side door. She didn't want to call attention to herself, so she resisted the urge and inched along with the crowd. She was relieved to find Brent waiting for her when she finally emerged.

"How much of that last phone conversation were you able to hear?" she asked.

"I'm not sure what you can get out of it, but Gene was

arguing with someone about money," Brent said. "It seemed like someone owed him money, or it didn't come the way it was supposed to, or something like that. Gene calmed down by the end of the conversation, as if the person he was talking with said something that satisfied him. I heard Gene say he would be by the next day to . . . to . . . take care of it? Do something. Oh, yes, pick it up. He said he would be by to pick it up."

Marge thanked Brent for waiting and for the information. "I'm not sure what it means, either, but it's another piece of the puzzle I'm trying to put together," she said.

Driving home, Marge wondered if Gene had gone to pick up whatever it was before he died. He was out most of the day and all evening, which was why Marge had finally gone to bed alone and awakened in the middle of the night to discover he still wasn't there. Perhaps what he had picked up was what got him killed. Which would mean he wasn't killed in the garage, wouldn't it? Or had he picked it up and come home, where someone was waiting for him?

Whatever the thing was, it wasn't in the car with him when he died. Or at least not by the time he was found.

Once Marge arrived home, she had no more time to think about it. Barely noticing the For Sale sign on the lawn, she hurried into the house to find seven messages awaited her. Before she could listen to all of them, more calls came in. Most of the people were looking for a steal not a deal. They lost interest as soon as they discovered Marge would not lower her price before they had at least seen the BMW. With every refusal to budge, her hope sank a little. How much would she eventually have to come down because the car was supposedly involved in a suicide?

One of the messages, though, was from the woman Melissa had mentioned. Marge returned this call first.

A tiny voice answered Marge's inquiry. "Yes, Charles Froyell is my attorney. Isn't he the dearest man? He held my hand through all the arrangements and decisions I had to make. I don't know what I would have done without him."

"Do you have children in the area?" Marge asked.

"No, my only son is grown and lives in New Mexico. He wasn't able to spend much time with me, but he checked everything out with Charles before he returned home after the funeral."

Marge didn't quite know how to put the next question. "And, uh, are all of your finances in good shape?" she finally got out, wincing at the blunt sound of it.

The line was silent for a moment. When the voice continued, it sounded guarded. "Why, yes. My husband left me adequately provided for. Why do you ask?"

Marge grasped at the first thing she could think of. "I'm considering Mr. Froyell as my attorney and want to be sure he is careful about the financial details," she said.

"Oh, yes." The woman's voice was bright again. "Charles is just wonderful. He treated me as if I were his mother. You will have no regrets about choosing him as your attorney. I'm so glad you called, so I could give him my vote of approval."

Marge hung up, disappointed not to have learned anything useful from the conversation. Although, even if Charles didn't always prey on the finances of his widowed clients, he seemed to play with their emotions.

Or, was that a perverse streak of jealousy about a woman probably old enough to be her mother? After all, wasn't it the attorney's job to take care of business for his clients and help them through the rough times?

As soon as she hung up the phone, the BMW calls started again, and prospective buyers arrived shortly thereafter. Marge was careful to take down each person's name before giving out her address. It was rather chilling when three callers hung up rather than give their names.

Marge looked and saw the Watsons' curtains swing back and forth every time a car drove in. She smiled when she visualized Willy fingering the handle of his baseball bat as he peered out the window.

"Oops," she said aloud, catching sight of the For Sale sign again. She hadn't yet told the Watsons or Lori she was selling the house. She was reluctant to leave while the phone was ringing so frequently. She'd have to make amends later.

Between calls, Marge looked around the house, trying to decide what items she would keep once it sold. She was sure she wouldn't need much. Maybe the kids would want some of the furniture. As soon as she had a few moments of silence, she called Robert.

"You're going to do what?" Robert's voice came out in a strained whisper. "But . . . but, Mother, that's our home. Dad's home. How can you sell it?"

"I can't afford to keep it."

"You know we'll help you—both Kate and I. I guess I was dreaming to think Caroline would agree to buy the house, but I don't want to lose our family home. Please, don't do this."

"Robert, you have your life to live and I have mine. This was a wonderful home for a family, but not for a single woman. The fact is I need the money and I don't intend to become dependent on my children. It's a done deal. It will do no good to try to talk me out of it."

Robert was silent so long Marge wondered if he was still on the line. When he finally spoke, his voice sounded dispirited. "I'd love to have the desk," Robert said. "I hate to lose all of Dad's favorite things. But I know Caroline won't agree to the desk, even if it would fit. She called it his ego prop."

"Well, talk to her about the rest of the furniture and other items," Marge said, annoyance rising at Caroline's harsh judgment of someone she didn't know that well. She had difficulty getting out the next words. "Do you think you could talk Caroline into coming over for dinner on Tuesday?"

"I don't know." He sounded doubtful. "I'll ask and see if she'll consider it."

When Marge phoned Kate, she discovered her daughter had already started planning for her move after graduation.

"Yesterday I found a great apartment downtown. It has a fantastic view of the sound. It's going to cost an arm and a leg to rent, but it is such an awesome location. I'll be moving in as soon as I finish my exams." Kate's voice was less enthusiastic when she added, after a long silence, "That is, unless you've changed your mind about my moving in with you."

Like father like daughter, Marge thought. She hadn't even passed the bar exam yet and she was already lining up the symbols that would declare her status and success.

Another long silence followed Marge's announcement that she was selling the house. When Kate finally spoke, the spark had gone out of her voice.

"I wish you didn't have to do this, Mom. It will be so hard not to have our house to come home to. It's almost like losing Dad all over again."

That nearly made Marge waver. But she knew she had to sell. It hurt now, but how much time would Kate and Robert actually spend here? Once they had children, they would have their own homes and lives. Marge knew she had to put her needs first, just as they did.

Kate said she'd come over Tuesday night. Marge found herself fearing the disappointment she would feel if Robert and Caroline didn't join them for what could possibly be their last family dinner in this house.

By three o'clock the calls tapered off so Marge took a chair outside to sit in the sun near the door. Wilma walked over, a thick mustard and ham sandwich in hand. Willy trailed close behind. "I'll bet you never took time for lunch before all those people started coming," she said. Marge was sure that curiosity about the Realtor's sign also had something to do with the treat.

"I listed the house for sale yesterday afternoon," she said, after chewing and swallowing a soul-satisfying bite. "I'm sorry I didn't have time to tell you before the sign went up."

"But, why?" Willy asked, his eyes filled with dismay.

"The house is too big for me alone," Marge said. "And, if I don't find our investment money, I'll need the proceeds from the sale to live on."

"It's such a shame," Wilma said. "Willy's work moved us around so much; I always thought how nice it would be to live in a friendly neighborhood for the rest of my life. Now, here I am, and my favorite neighbor is leaving. If only Gene had had life insurance."

Marge threw her arms around Wilma and gave her a huge hug. "You have been the best neighbors anyone could wish for," she said. "I'll miss you most of all when I move, but I'll come back to visit."

Another potential car buyer arrived, so the Watsons retreated to their house while Marge carried on. She had just found a few moments to polish off the sandwich when she looked up to see Bruce's BMW pull into her driveway. When he emerged from the car, he looked immaculate, as if he had just stepped out of the display window of an REI clothing store. A very young and very blonde woman emerged from the passenger side.

"I thought that was your phone number in the ad," Bruce said as he sauntered over to inspect Gene's BMW. "Gene took excellent care of it, didn't he? Looks like you cleaned it up nicely, too."

Marge's eyes narrowed. Why was Bruce so interested in Gene's BMW?

"Mindy is looking for a car and thought she'd like to have one like mine," he said, as if reading Marge's mind. "I assured her she couldn't afford it but, since we were out, we stopped by to take a look."

Bruce's wife divorced him shortly after he and Gene started the business. Marge had thought Bruce's wife was as unhappy about the new business as Marge and had less patience to deal with it. Now she wondered if that was all there was to the separation.

Mindy's eyes were all over the car while her hands traveled all over Bruce. "I bet with a little help I could manage it," she crooned.

Bruce laughed, making Marge start. She couldn't recall ever hearing Bruce laugh. Even now it didn't sound much like a laugh, more like a humorless bark. "Not on your life, baby." He turned to Marge, serious again. "How's it going?"

Marge shrugged. "No one wants to pay what it's worth; but I'll hold out a while longer," she said. Bruce looked at her as if that wasn't what he meant, but Marge ignored him. If she were inclined to confide her problems to Bruce, she wouldn't do it in front of his bimbo.

"Oh, by the way," she said, "I didn't think to look at the date on that receipt Gene gave you. What day was it exactly that you gave him the check?" she asked.

Bruce looked startled, as she had intended. If he had something to hide and she could catch him unaware, he might let something slip.

"I believe it was right after the new partner joined the firm," he said, the friendly banter gone from his voice. "Why do you ask?"

His reaction wasn't enough to tell Marge anything. She decided to avoid putting him on guard, in case she needed to approach him again. "I need to follow up to find out what Gene did with it. That narrows down the time frame for me. Thanks."

Before Marge finished speaking, Bruce was edging Mindy back to his car. Mindy seemed to have a hard time keeping her hands off Bruce. Perhaps she still thought she could persuade him in the heat of passion, but Marge was sure Mindy would be disappointed. Bruce's weakness was not physical passion.

Was it money? Who had said they saw Bruce in the casino?

By late afternoon, Marge's body sagged. Selling the BMW was harder than the packing and loading of boxes she had done last week. She was just deciding whether to have an early dinner and relax when Lori called.

"I'm all by myself tonight," she said. "Want to join me for dinner?"

The weariness evaporated. "Love to," Marge said. "I'll bring the wine." It wasn't until after she hung up that she wondered if there had been something different about Lori's voice. The thought vanished as she dashed out of the house, the door slamming behind her.

The light brightened in the Watsons' window. Marge waved. Had her neighbors always kept such close track of her coming and going? But, that was exactly what she had asked them to do after advertising the BMW for sale. It was comforting to know they took the request so seriously.

Lori normally looked as together in jeans and a flannel shirt as she did in her workday clothes. Unlike Caroline, who made a statement with her sharp suits and stiletto heels, Lori's office attire tended toward comfortable dressy loafers or low-heeled pumps with softly tailored suits and dresses.

Tonight, however, Lori's easy assurance was missing. Her smile, as she greeted Marge, was shaky. She seemed to lose her place while opening the wine and pouring a glass for each of them. She stopped and looked around the room, as if trying to remember what she was doing.

Marge waited as long as she could. When Lori brought the wine to the table and sat down, Marge exclaimed, "Lori, something is wrong. What is it? Can you talk to me about it?"

Lori burst into tears. "I think Frank is going to leave me."

Marge gripped the stem of her wine glass so hard she thought it might break. Of all the things she might have expected, this wasn't it. She carefully set the glass on the table. "What makes you think that?" she asked.

"He's been going on so many business trips lately," Lori said. "And he's been so distracted; I suspected he was having an affair. Then," she added, struggling to get control of her voice, "I found out he has done something with most of our money."

Marge was glad she wasn't still holding the glass. She didn't think it would withstand the force of her grip. She swallowed over a lump in her throat.

"How much money are you talking about?"

"I don't know. I know he cashed in at least a hundred thousand worth of mutual funds and another fifty thousand in treasury bills. I found the statements for both of those today, but no record of what he did with the money. Since the boys are almost finished with school, that money was supposed to go into our retirement fund."

Marge rose and walked behind the chair, so Lori couldn't see her face, trying to keep her growing concern under control. She put her hands on Lori's shoulders and gave what she hoped was a reassuring squeeze. "Don't assume Frank is having an affair or leaving you. He might have found an irresistible investment for that money, like Gene did."

Lori sat upright. "I'd rather it was that—even if we lose all our money. But, that doesn't explain the sudden increase in so-called business trips or his distraction."

"Maybe not the trips, but if Frank has begun to suspect something is wrong with his investment, it could explain the distraction. When does he return from this trip?"

The tears came back again. "That's why I think he might have left me. He said he would be gone at least two weeks— Frank has never been away that long before and he always knows exactly when he's coming back. But, for the last few months, he hardly says anything about where he is going or why."

"Can you call his office?"

"He'd never forgive me if I'm wrong and he found out. What reason could I give for asking where my husband is and what he is doing? Besides, Frank makes his own schedule and just tells them where he will be and when."

"Maybe you could tell his office you lost the information he gave you about where he was staying. Then you could get the name of the hotel and a phone number."

"I probably could. But then what? Frank doesn't expect a call because he didn't give me that information. Do I ring up and say, 'Are you having an affair? And, by the way, what did you do with our money?'"

Marge moved around so she could look into Lori's eyes, willing Lori to understand the importance of what she was about to say. "Lori, you have to find some way to do this. Gene evidently never told anyone who talked him out of his money. If, by chance, Frank has made the same investment, he knows the name of the person. That would be enough to get the police to act and maybe even accept that Gene was murdered because of it. In the process, we might keep Frank from putting himself in the same position Gene was in, and we may be able to get the money back for both of us."

"All right," Lori said, though her reluctance was evident. "Tomorrow morning I'll call Frank's office and see what I can find out. Right after I phone our lawyer and make sure Frank hasn't started divorce proceedings or something."

"Who is your lawyer?" Marge asked.

"Charles Froyell, in Bellevue."

Marge stared. "Lori, do me a big favor. Don't call Charles until after you've talked to Frank. Give Frank the benefit of the doubt."

And, thought Marge, don't let Charles know you suspect something is wrong. It could be the biggest mistake you ever make. Even if Charles doesn't rip off every woman he deals with, he might have found a way to take advantage of more than one.

CHAPTER 8

~

THEY MANAGED A quick dinner. Lori tried to keep up her end of the conversation but had to stop whenever her voice choked with tears. After eating, Marge went home.

As soon as the door closed, Marge felt the loneliness envelop her and seep into her bones. It was easy to be brave when she was busy in the middle of the day. How could she live through the long nights?

"One at a time," Gene's voice assured her. "One at a time."

She grimaced, irritated at the easy assurance. "If you can talk to me, why can't you tell me what happened to the money? Show me where to start looking. Explain how I'm supposed to go on living without you," she cried.

No answer came.

Perhaps what she thought was Gene's voice was only her

subconscious telling her what she already knew. The thought depressed her. She had begun to look forward to hearing Gene's voice . . . perhaps one day to know that he forgave her.

Monday morning arrived softly, the sun having retreated again behind a thin sheet of gray clouds. Marge woke early and lay in bed for a few minutes, weighted down by the silence. Eventually she forced herself out of bed, turned on the radio, started the coffee, and showered and dressed.

With her first cup of coffee in hand, she marched into the office to try the telephone numbers she had found in Gene's drawer on Saturday. Staying busy was the only way to defeat the quiet. She started with the employment agencies.

As she suspected, Gene contacted them two months before he died, which had to be before he knew his illness was terminal. The information they provided was similar to what she had received on Friday.

The Dorsey and Company investment agency was hesitant to give out any information. The receptionist passed her on to an agent, who finally turned her over to a broker, who asked a lot of questions to establish that Marge was who she said she was.

"My name is Carl Higgely," he said, once he was convinced. "Your husband dealt with me. I read about his death in the *Times*. I am sorry to hear about your loss."

"What was it that Gene came to you for?" Marge asked. "I thought he was happy with our investments."

"Actually, he wasn't interested in investing. He called me about five weeks ago seeking information about an investment he had already made in a limited partnership. I knew of the company; limited partnerships are somewhat risky for the type of situation Gene described, but this particular partnership has proven management and has done very well over the last five years. It probably would have given you a nice income. By the time the partnership might dissolve, you would have been in a position to plan your own financial security.

"I told your husband something must be wrong when he said he had received no confirmation or any type of correspondence from the company. He asked how he could go about getting the company investigated. I told him I didn't think there was anything wrong with the company itself. More likely it was the investment broker who handled the transaction. But he insisted; so I gave him the name of a firm that looks into possible investment scams."

"Did Gene say what broker he used?"

"No. I asked, but he said he didn't want to smear anyone's reputation before he had all the facts."

That sounded like Gene. "Have you ever heard of a Cheltington Investment Company?"

"No, but I'll check and see if such a company exists. I'll get back to you on that."

"I didn't find the investigator's name among Gene's personal effects," Marge said. "Could you give it to me? Along with the name of the company he invested in?"

"Certainly. Just a moment while I get that information."

Marge wrote down the names and phone numbers before thanking Carl profusely. She finally had something to work with. She had the Cheltington Investment Company from the endorsement on the checks. She had a limited partnership called the Cypress Hills Development Company, where the money was to be invested. And, she had Glenn Investigations, who might be able to supply a few more of the pieces she needed.

Was the money invested late, after Gene started checking on it? Who ran the Cheltington Investment Company? If the money hadn't been invested, what did Cheltington do with it? And what did any of this have to do with Gene's death?

Marge had to field a few calls about the BMW before she could phone Glenn Investigations.

"That was Mr. Glenn's case," the secretary informed Marge. "He is out of the office this morning. However, I know he finished that investigation several weeks ago and sent a report to his client."

Marge shook her head. He sent Gene the report already? What happened to it? "Is there any way I can get a copy of the report?" Marge asked.

"I can't send you one without Mr. Glenn's authorization. You'll have to wait until he returns to the office."

"When will he be back?"

"I'm not sure. He didn't know how long it would take to complete his business today."

"Would you please leave him a message, asking him to call me the moment he gets back? I must get a copy of that report immediately."

The receptionist took Marge's name and number and promised to give Mr. Glenn the message when he came in.

Disappointed, Marge hung up the phone. She had found no trace of the report while cleaning the house. Of course, since Gene was hiding the truth from her he would have made sure it was somewhere she wouldn't find it. Maybe it was in the BMW. Even though the kids cleaned the car inside and out, and Brian brought her that slip of paper, maybe they left something in the car assuming it belonged there. She went out to the driveway and started searching the BMW.

Nothing remained in the interior except the expected manuals in the glove compartment and a faint, unpleasant odor that concerned her. The smell was not acceptable in a luxury car. How was she going to get rid of it? Marge finished with the interior and opened the trunk, when Willy came out of the house next door.

"You can't have sold it already," he said.

"No, not yet. Just looking for something."

"I thought the kids cleaned it out."

"It looks like they did." Marge lifted the mat and checked around the edges of the trunk. "It isn't here." She closed the trunk and turned to Willy. "I think Gene invested our money. He had an investigation done into some investment he made. But, I can't find a copy of the investigator's report or any clue as to how to find the firm he used to make the investment."

Willy looked startled. "Now, why would he keep paperwork like that in the trunk of his car?" He hugged Marge quickly and hard, nearly dislocating her shoulder. "Don't you think Gene would have shared the results of any report with you?"

"Yes, I would have thought he would," Marge said, rubbing her shoulder and wondering again why Gene hadn't. "Well, anyway, it's not here. I'll have to wait until the investigator returns so I can get a copy of the report."

Willy stayed by the car, staring after her as she escaped into the house. Wilma would probably be over within half an hour with gingerbread cookies.

A prospective buyer for the BMW arrived with his mechanic. "I'll give you sixteen thousand," he said after his mechanic had checked the car and left. Marge hesitated. That was well below the wholesale book value.

"It's worth far more than that," she managed to say. "In

the condition it's in, I could get twenty for it, easy." Marge wanted to take the words back as soon as she said them. That was less than retail book value, and she might have to settle for it. She hadn't meant to set it as the top of a bargaining range.

Marge needn't have feared the buyer would take her up on it. "Oh, come on," he said, peering at her with a condescending grin, "surely you don't expect to get that much for *this* car."

Marge glared at the man. "What I know is I can get what this car is worth," she stated. "And I know it's worth more than sixteen thousand—even to a dealer, even *this* car. So, if that is the best offer you can make, the answer is no. Thank you for your interest."

She turned on her heels to go. "Well, what will you take for it?" the buyer called after her, evidently realizing he did not have the upper hand.

"More than you want to pay," Marge snapped and went into the house, slamming the door behind her. Even if she ended up selling it to a dealer for less than sixteen thousand dollars, she wouldn't sell it to a chauvinist idiot.

The phone was ringing again and there were two messages on the answering machine. There followed a virtual onslaught of inquiries and visitors. She wouldn't have thought there could be this many BMW buyers in a city the size of Bellevue. And, in reality, there weren't. Many of the so-called buyers seemed more interested in trying to pry details of the suicide from Marge than purchasing a car. By midmorning, Marge was ready to give it up and take whatever she could get from the dealer.

Shortly before noon, a car and a truck drove up together. A man obviously dressed for the office stepped out of the Mercedes and approached Marge.

"My name is David Walters," he said. He waved towards a man emerging from the truck. "I hope you don't mind. I knew if your BMW was as good as it sounded it would go fast, so I brought my mechanic with me."

Marge could only nod, her mouth cottony. Was it possible he didn't know about Gene? What would he think when he got a whiff of the interior? Did she have to tell him?

Marge watched David Walters during the inspection and as he consulted with the mechanic. He appeared to be about Gene's age. She noted his medium-brown hair, slightly long but neatly trimmed and beginning to gray around the temples. Like Gene's.

"How does nineteen thousand dollars sound?" he asked.

"A little low," she answered, trying to sound assured while her heart thumped. "I don't need a mechanic to tell me there may not be another used BMW in the city in this good of condition. It was my husband's baby, and it always had to be perfect."

"Well, you're right about that," the man admitted, startling Marge. "That's why I'm interested. I want something special for my daughter who is graduating from college. I like this car because for a used car price I can get something classy that I won't have to worry about her driving." The man's gray-blue eyes lit up when he spoke of his daughter, and a smile crinkled the corners of his mouth while showing a set of remarkably even teeth. Marge's head swam. The look in those eyes mirrored Gene's when he spoke proudly of Kate and her accomplishments.

The mechanic called Mr. Walters over and talked to him quietly for a moment. When Mr. Walters came back, there was a slight furrow in his brow.

"Mrs. Christensen, may I offer my condolences on the loss of your husband. That must have been very difficult."

Marge nodded numbly, not knowing what to say.

"My mechanic tells me it will take some work and money to get rid of the slight odor inside the car, but he's sure he can do it. And, he wants to check to see if the engine needs any work. Because of that, I think the nineteen thousand will have to be my final offer."

Marge was so startled she almost shook her head. He was still willing to buy it. Should she hold out to try to find a buyer who would pay more? She didn't want to risk it. She might lose a fair offer.

"I think you have a deal," she said. She swallowed hard. Had he thought it through? Could she risk losing the sale by raising a concern? When she spoke again, her voice was barely audible. "If you're sure your daughter will have no problem driving it after . . . after what happened."

"If my mechanic is as good as he says—and experience indicates he is—she will never have to know. But, even if she does find out, I don't think she'd have a problem with it. My daughter is an extremely down-to-earth and practical young lady." He smiled again.

Marge sighed in relief. "How do you plan to pay for it?"

"I'll come by tomorrow with a cashier's check."

When David Walters left and Marge turned to go into the house, she noticed the curtain flutter in the Watsons' window. She had to tell them right away, but first . . . she carefully closed the door behind her, jabbed her fists in the air, and twirled around the entranceway nearly knocking a picture off the wall, and finally letting out a whoop the Watsons probably heard. She had the money she needed to keep going for . . .

Marge stopped spinning and tried to figure out how long she could live on nineteen thousand dollars. She knew she could support herself on much less than Gene and she had, but many things were going on and she had no idea what unexpected expenses might arise.

The phone rang. "I'm sorry, the car has already been sold," Marge replied to the caller. After hanging up, she rigged Gene's fancy answering machine with a message stating that the BMW had been sold and instructing the caller to leave a message if the phone call was for another purpose.

"I am so glad, dear." Wilma Watson's round face lit up when Marge ran next door to announce the sale. "You needed to get that awful reminder out of your life. And now you have a small nest egg to get you started." She took off to find Willy and tell him the good news.

When Wilma returned with Willy, Marge hesitated before saying, "Come over to my house for a minute. I want you to hear something."

They trooped across the driveways to Marge's house.

"When I hooked up Gene's answering machine a couple of days ago, I found this message on it. It seems like I should know the voice, but I can't figure it out. Does it ring any bells with you?"

She played the message twice. Wilma looked almost comical with a look of deep concentration on her face. "No, I don't think I ever heard the voice before," she said. "What about you, Willy?"

Willy shook his head, looking dazed. "First the investment report is missing, and now this," he said. "Your digging seems to be paying off, Marge."

"What do you think it means?" Wilma asked.

"I think it means Gene definitely invested our money somewhere. But, the investigation report I told you about earlier, Willy, makes me think something was wrong and Gene was trying to straighten it out. He evidently didn't get it finished, though, before he died."

"I didn't know your money was gone until you told me about the investigation," Willy said, his voice soft and thoughtful. "Do you think that is why Gene killed himself?"

"Oh, no. I don't think he killed himself at all," Marge said. "I think it was rigged to look that way because someone was afraid Gene would figure everything out and go to the police."

Willy and Wilma both stared at her, their eyes matching circles of blue.

"Oh, Marge," Wilma cried. "You need to accept what the police said about how Gene died. That's the only way you can get over his death and go on with your life."

"Never," Marge said firmly. "Someone killed Gene and I'm not going to stop searching until I find out who it was."

Weariness descended on Marge after they left. She prepared herself a salad for lunch and tried to rest, but she was too keyed up to relax. Now that the BMW was sold she had to get the house ready to sell.

Unable to sit still, she cleaned out the coat closet. When she was finished, she had no more clues; but she did have another box of clothes for Goodwill. She had barely finished packing the box when the phone rang. She let it ring until the answering machine ran its spiel. She quickly grabbed the receiver when she heard Melissa's voice.

"I have a prospective buyer who wants to see your house at about six o'clock today. Does that work for you? I'd also like to put up a lockbox, so we can show the house when you aren't home."

"Sure," Marge said, hardly hearing the comment about the lockbox. Prospective buyers already? She wasn't ready.

In a daze, Marge stowed the box of coats in the Honda and made a quick walk through the house to clear away any obvious clutter. Before she had finished her inspection, the phone rang again.

"Mrs. Christensen? This is Gregory Glenn, from Glenn Investigations."

Marge thought her heart would stop beating. "Yes, this is Marge Christensen."

"I understand you are interested in a report I prepared for your late husband. My condolences on your loss. I read about his death in the *Times*."

"Thank you, Mr. Glenn." Marge wondered if it was possible to make the stock phrase of condolence sound any colder. She replied in kind, "How do I go about getting a copy of the report?"

"I sent your husband the report almost six weeks ago, but I was never paid for the investigation."

"My husband must have died before . . ."

"As I said, I am sorry for your loss, Mrs. Christensen, but I can't afford to work for free. I will need payment for the report and the copy before I can send it to you."

"How much will that be?" Marge asked. Tears she refused to shed stung her eyes. No one, not even the police, had been so cold to her about Gene's death.

"A thousand dollars for the investigation and original report, and fifty dollars for the copy." He paused a moment. "No, make that a flat thousand. I don't want to make you pay for a copy since it appears you never saw the original."

Marge swallowed hard. So generous—a fifty dollar break. A thousand dollars was a big chunk out of her paltry assets, which looked so large a short while ago. Was it too much? It didn't matter if it was. She had to have the report.

"Where shall I send the check? Or can I pick it up?"

"No need to come to the office. The report won't be

mailed until the check clears." Another pause. "I'm sorry, Mrs. Christensen. I realize that sounds harsh in your circumstances, but it will only add a day before you get it and it is company policy since the original payment was never received." He gave her the address and hung up.

"Company policy means *your* policy," Marge mumbled as she went to the desk to write out a check. She supposed she couldn't blame him. He said it only took a day for the check to clear; but how could she wait even one extra day, knowing the report might give her the answers she sought?

She could cut the mail time, though. Writing out the check and grabbing her purse, Marge ran to the Honda. She'd drive the check to the Glenn Investigation offices in Seattle. She looked at her watch. She should be back before Melissa showed the house.

Marge dropped off the box of coats at Goodwill before driving across the floating bridge into Seattle. She splurged on a parking garage rather than taking the time to look for a street meter. As a result, she made it back home in plenty of time to let Melissa and her client in. Marge left again while they viewed the house.

Most women she knew filled in any spare hours they could find at the Bellevue Square Shopping Center. Marge had no interest in looking at items she wasn't prepared to buy. And she couldn't quiet her thoughts enough to enjoy a book at the library. So, on a sudden impulse, she stopped at an art supply store and purchased a sketchpad and charcoal drawing pencil.

She found a parking spot near a small park with benches, pulled a jacket around her shoulders, and sat on a bench facing a bed of early spring flowers. But her pencil didn't draw the flowers. Instead, what emerged on the paper was Gene's face, in profile, as she had seen it when he was standing on that balcony. Her fingers would never forget. With deft strokes she shadowed his square jaw line and drew out the intensity of his dark eyes as they stared into the distance. What had been going on behind those eyes? When did he plan on opening up to her?

Marge was amazed to discover over an hour had passed by the time she finished the sketch. Returning to the Honda, she turned on the heat and waited for it to warm her before driving home. She slowed when she neared her driveway, in case Melissa's client was still there; but Melissa's car was alone in the driveway and Melissa was busy installing a lockbox near the front door.

"Do you have time for a cup of coffee or a glass of wine?" Marge asked.

"I have an appointment back at the office tonight, so no wine; but I'd love a cup of coffee. Just let me get this done first. Do you have a spare key I can put in it?"

Marge went upstairs to where she had always kept a spare key hidden away, much to Gene's amusement. He said he thought they might change the locks if someone lost a key, but Marge had used the spare more than once for visitors who needed to come and go on their own schedules. In a few minutes, Melissa was finished with the lockbox and joined Marge at the kitchen table.

"Tell me, is there anything I need to do to make sure the house is ready for showing?" Marge asked when they were seated in front of steaming mugs.

"Well, to tell the truth, I think you should get rid of that big desk and convert that room back into a dining room. It's amazing how hard it is for some people to visualize a room differently than they see it. And, that wall of shelves makes the room look smaller. Other than that, I think the house is in great shape."

Marge shook her head. "I should have been able to figure that out for myself," she said.

"Don't be silly. You're going through so much, I'm amazed you can think straight. Look at how much you have accomplished. How are you doing on the sale of the BMW?"

Marge was startled. She had forgotten she told Melissa about selling the car and why, but she was even more surprised Melissa remembered that detail from a client's life.

"Done," Marge said with a grin. "I'll finalize it and get the check tomorrow."

"That must feel good," Melissa said.

"I'll put an ad in the paper tomorrow, to sell the desk," Marge said, feeling like she was on a roll and needed to keep going. "My children are coming over tomorrow night to pick out what furniture they want. That is, if my daughter-in-law decides to come."

Melissa looked at her. "I sense a problem. Anything you want to talk about?"

Marge reviewed the recent scene with Robert and Caroline and the history of animosity between Caroline and her. "I must be missing something. I can't seem to find what Robert sees in Caroline and I haven't had any luck in getting her to see the real me," Marge said. "I know that doesn't make much sense, but I don't know how else to explain it."

"It makes perfect sense," Melissa said. "May I make one small suggestion?"

"Certainly. I'll take all the help I can get."

"Don't talk to her through your son. Talk to Caroline directly. Ask her if she wants anything from the house."

Marge slapped her forehead and raised her eyes to the ceiling. Of course, that was exactly what she had done. Because of her discomfort at Caroline's apparent dislike, she didn't deal with her directly. All her communication was with and through Robert.

"How did you get to be so smart?" she asked Melissa.

"Well, I wasn't born that way," Melissa said with a rueful smile. "In fact, I'm not usually that smart when it comes to my own life. But, I'll let you continue to think I am."

They laughed and began exchanging life histories. Melissa was from Idaho, a late baby in a family of four older brothers. "Though our father died when I was very young, I still had four father figures looking out for me," she said. "Most of the time, I could wrap any of them around my little finger. But, when they all decided something was right or wrong for me, they stood together like a brick wall. That's why, as much as I love them, I have to live so far away."

Marge felt a pang of disappointment when Melissa glanced at her watch and jumped up. "Sorry to leave so abruptly," she said. "I'll barely make my next appointment if I rush. Thank you for the coffee and the conversation."

As soon as Melissa left, Marge went to the phone to call Caroline. "Caroline? Hello, this is Marge," she said, careful not to say Mother, since Caroline never called her that. Actually, Caroline had never called her anything. Maybe she didn't know what to call her.

"Yes?" Caroline replied in her crisp, cool voice.

"I wanted to let you know," Marge said, trying to slightly emphasize the you without making it too obvious, "that you are welcome to anything from the house you might want for your new place. Kate is coming over tomorrow evening and I hope you are coming over, too."

The line was silent. "I will be decorating our home in a modern style," Caroline finally said, "so I don't think anything from the house will fit in. However, I'll talk with

Robert about it. And, we already decided to come over tomorrow."

Her words were as cold as ever, Marge thought as she hung up. But, at least her family would be gathered tomorrow night.

Knowing that neither Kate nor Robert wanted it and feeling flush with her success at selling the BMW, Marge went to clean out the desk so she could place an ad in the *Bellevue Journal American* in the morning.

An hour later, the desk was empty. Marge found no more slips of paper, no unfamiliar bank books, no leads to Gene's activities over the last two months of his life, and no report from the investigation firm. Putting tax returns and other important papers aside for the moment, she grabbed mineral oil and a soft cloth and gave the desk a good cleaning and polishing.

Since Robert's was the only other desk in the house, Marge decided to put the papers there. She could find another place if Robert and Caroline decided they wanted it. As long as she was in a cleaning mood, she decided to tackle the stuck drawer and clean that desk, too.

When Marge crawled under the desk to work the drawer loose, she discovered the problem was too much stuff wedged in the drawer. It took nearly an hour of jiggling and finagling to free the drawer. When it finally pulled open, she dumped the contents on top of the desk, soaped the runners as a precaution, and slid the drawer in and out a few times to make sure it was intact and in good working order. Finally, she sorted through the stack on the desk.

Along with the pens, paper clips, and other expected paraphernalia, were a bunch of Robert's old school papers. After Marge had read and discarded most of them she was left with a blank, creased, and slightly torn envelope full of neatly folded paper. This was the culprit that had jammed the drawer.

Marge pulled the papers out of the envelope and unfolded them. She stared at the top sheet, her head swimming.

It was Gene's handwriting . . . it said something about their funds.

CHAPTER 9

~

MARGE HELD THE papers in shaking hands. She closed her eyes, envisioning Gene secreting the papers away in the drawer, afraid to believe that she had found the answer to what happened to him.

When she steadied her hands, she opened her eyes and smoothed the papers into a neat pile. She drew a deep breath and started to read the first one. Gene had drawn a line down the middle to divide the page into two columns. In the first column he listed their Stock Fund and Bond Fund. In the second column he entered $466,300 and $137,600; the approximate value of each of the mutual funds, then the total $603,900. Below that he multiplied the total by 8%, getting $48,312.

Tears blurred Marge's vision. She closed her eyes and imagined Gene sitting at Robert's desk, probably in the middle of the night while she was sleeping, running figures to make sure she would have enough to live on after he died. "Oh, Gene, forgive me for doubting you," she whispered through the tears.

She wiped her eyes and went on to the next page. If he had found an investment that paid a steady 8%, she could have lived pretty well on $48,312 a year, plus whatever she earned working or through her art.

Gene had divided the second page into three columns. In the first column he listed Present Investment, Treasury Bills and CDs, and Cypress Hills. In the second he entered what Marge assumed were the percentages he projected each investment would return, 6%, 5%, and 8% respectively. The resulting figures in the third column were $36,234; $30,195; and $48,312.

Even with the percentages of the first two figured high, if Cypress Hills was correct, the next-best return was more than $12,000 less per year. Remembering the missing report, Marge rifled quickly through the pages and double-checked everything she had taken from the desk. It wasn't there.

The third page was dated six weeks ago—two weeks before Gene's death and around the time Charles said Gene closed out the mutual funds. On the line after the date it read: Cypress Hills Development Company. On the line after that: Initial Investment $603,900.

Had he found some way to avoid taxes, maybe he planned on paying them with the money from the business? Or did he have other funds with which to pay them? He skipped a line, wrote a date in June, skipped another line, and wrote a date in September, and after a few more lines, he wrote December. He was prepared for tracking quarterly dividends. It looked like Gene had already made the investment.

Halfway down the page, Gene had written Business Investment Growth. After the figure $200,000 (E) was another set of quarterly dates. Marge nearly stopped breathing. What did (E) mean? Did it mean Gene wasn't sure how much it would be, indicating he didn't have the money—or an accounting of it yet? Or maybe he had the money but he didn't know how much would have to go for taxes?

She quickly turned to the last page. It appeared to be a to-do list. The first four items were checked off, the last four she suspected were added after the first ones had been completed.

1. Check with broker ✔
2. Bank for cancelled check ✔
3. Confront Nb ✔
4. Get independent report on Cypress Hills ✔
5. Confront Nb again?
6. Call Charles Froyell
7. Lawsuit ????
8. Police ????

Did Gene ever call Charles? He hadn't checked off that item. What did Nb stand for? Number? If so, what did he mean by "confront it"? If they were initials, why was the b lower case? Maybe Gene talked with Charles, but didn't get it checked off. Marge picked up the phone. If Gene had spoken with Charles it could have been the last conversation he had before he died. And, if he had forgotten to check it off the list, then he might have also forgotten to check off the second Nb. If Gene hadn't talked with Charles, then the first Nb contact could be the last one he had. After six rings she heard the answering machine click on.

"Charles, this is Marge," she said. "I need to speak to you as soon as possible. Please call me immediately."

Chewing her lip, Marge hung up and stared at the list. Gene, always bending over backwards to be fair, had made sure no one could accidentally discover who he suspected until he had proof. And, it sounded like Frank was doing the same thing. It had cost Gene his life—she hoped the similarity would not go that far with Frank.

She stood and began to pace around the house, staring at the list as she did so. She should show it to Detective Peterson. Would he consider it evidence and take it away from her?

She grabbed her keys and ran to the car, surprised to discover it was dark. She clutched the papers in the hand she waved toward Wilma and Willy, who stood in their doorway watching as she drove out.

When Marge returned with two sets of pages, she could find no safe place downstairs to keep them. Even though no one knew she had them, she felt nervous about the chance of their being seen. She returned upstairs and put one set back in Robert's desk drawer and the other in her dresser.

He wouldn't confront Nebraska? New Brunswick? No, dummy, you don't confront a place. It had to be a person. Nolan Bryant. Wasn't he a TV personality? Ned B . . . Nelson B . . . Nathan B . . . Nancy B . . . Nelly B . . . Nora B . . . But how could a woman have managed to kill Gene and make it look like suicide? Unless she had help?

Where was Gene's voice when she needed it?

She picked up the phone and dialed Lori's number.

"I haven't been able to reach Frank," Lori said, her voice so faint Marge had difficulty hearing her. "I got the number from his office, but he either hasn't been at the hotel or he isn't returning my call."

"Don't jump to conclusions," Marge said, struggling to keep the impatience out of her voice. "I'm sure he is busy with work and will return your call as soon as he has a chance."

It was all Marge could do to keep from throwing the phone across the room when she hung up. If Frank could give her the information she needed, she might be able to resolve the whole affair. How long would it be before he got back to Lori?

Suddenly feeling bereft, she grabbed one of Gene's sweatshirts and put it on, hugging its warm comfort. She threw together a tomato and lettuce sandwich and ate slowly. Tired of puttering around the house, she got out her new sketchpad. She doodled for a few minutes, when the pencil started moving of its own volition. Before Marge knew it, she was looking at a small likeness of David Walters, his eyes alight with the gentle shine that came when he talked about his daughter. Where did that come from?

She shivered and hugged Gene's sweatshirt tighter, staring at the sketch, feeling disloyal. Marge tore it off the pad. She was about to wad the page and throw it away when inspiration struck. The sketch would make a lovely surprise gift for David's daughter.

Taking off the sweatshirt, she went to Robert's room to rummage through her supplies for a frame and matting and spent the next hour putting it all together. When it was finished, she wrapped it and put it on the front seat of the BMW. She had written "David's daughter" on the wrapping in the hopes that it would stay there until the girl could discover it herself.

She sat down again with the sketchpad. This time Gene's face came to her clearly. It was the same pensive pose she remembered from the party in Newport Hills—only tonight Marge could see the pain in his eyes, the slight frown on his brow. She didn't try to hold back her tears.

How could she ever have doubted Gene? Why had she never seen what he was going through? Why was she off trying to find some elusive happiness of her own when he needed her?

She found another frame and put the drawing on her dresser before going to bed.

Sleep didn't come easily. The house was too quiet. When she did drift off, images of Gene reaching out overwhelmed her. She wanted to reach back, to hold him and comfort him, but her arms felt tied down to the bed.

"I'm sorry, Gene," she whispered.

She felt a hand rest against her forehead, felt a wave of forgiveness flow through her.

"You will find out what happened," she heard Gene's voice say. Eventually, she fell asleep.

When David arrived before noon, Marge, sleeves rolled up, was in the middle of polishing the kitchen floor tiles.

"Mr. Walters, come in," she said, automatically reaching up to smooth her hair.

"David, please," he replied. He stared at her for a moment and Marge felt her face flush. She turned away to hide the redness. David seemed to recover himself and looked around appreciatively as they walked through the hall to the kitchen. "If I weren't already set where I am, I'd buy this place in a heartbeat," he said. "You have a lovely home, and you've maintained it as well as the car."

"Thank you," she said. "Would you like a cup of coffee?"

"If it's no trouble. I could use a break this morning." He sat at the table and quickly signed the paperwork. "If you have the keys available, I have someone outside ready to take the car." After he had delivered the keys, he relaxed in the chair and cradled his coffee mug in his hands.

"Are you going to wait for graduation to present the car to your daughter? That's still a month or so off, isn't it?"

"About six weeks, yes. I've rented a garage near my office to stow it until the big day." His eyes had that glow again. Marge had to swallow the lump that formed in her throat.

"Too bad she's finishing with college, otherwise you might also want the big desk I'm trying to sell," she said.

David laughed. "No, unfortunately, the next gift I'll be buying for her will probably be a wedding gift. I was hoping she'd go on to graduate school, and she still may, but she became engaged two weeks ago. I expect them to announce the date of the wedding right after her graduation. Do you have children?"

"A son and a daughter. My son is married and is an accountant. His wife is a retail-clothing buyer. My daughter is graduating from law school this year and has a job already. I can't believe how grown and independent she is. Have you and your wife met your daughter's fiancé?"

The clear eyes clouded. "My wife passed away two years ago. Cancer." Marge could see the visible effort to contain his emotions and regretted that she had brought it up. Two years. How long would it be before her heart didn't sink every time she thought of Gene?

"I've met Ken," he added, "and it looks like my daughter has made a good choice. But, it is hard not being the Most Important Man in her life anymore." The eyes crinkled into laughter again.

David paused at the door when he was about to leave. "Do you have a second set of keys to the car?"

Marge's mind momentarily went blank. "Oh, of course." She had been using her set of keys for the BMW and had forgotten about Gene's. She turned to the key holder near the garage door. There were no keys hanging there. She went to the dining room to look through Gene's desk only to stand in confusion, shaking her head. Of course there was nothing in the desk. Asking David to wait a moment, she ran upstairs and checked all the drawers, then came back down and rummaged through the kitchen.

"I'm sorry, I can't find my husband's keys," she said. "Either my son or . . . or someone must have them." Marge almost bit her tongue when she nearly blurted out that the police might have them.

"No problem," David assured her. "When you find them, let me know and I'll come pick them up."

Marge was relieved he trusted her enough to do that. As he was leaving the house, David paused and pulled out a business card and a pen. He quickly jotted a phone number on the back and handed it to her. "For when you find the keys. Also, if you ever need anything, please give me a call. That's my home number on the back. I think I know what you are going through, and sometimes it feels good to have a sympathetic ear available."

Marge ducked her head to hide the quick tears that came to her eyes. "Thank you," she managed to say before she closed the door and leaned against it, trembling.

She needed another cup of coffee before she could finish waxing the kitchen floor.

A few moments later, Robert phoned. "Mom, what did you say to Caroline?"

Marge hesitated before answering. Had she erred in calling? Had she said something wrong despite trying to be so careful? "I invited her to look over the house furnishings to see if there was anything she wanted."

"Well, thank you," he said. "She's still cool with me, but she agreed we can join you for dinner tonight."

"Great. We'll do a cookout if the weather permits."

"Mom . . . thanks again."

"Oh, Robert," Marge said, remembering just in time. "Do you have your father's set of keys? I can't find them anywhere."

"No, I never saw them. Maybe the police took them and forgot to give them back."

"Okay, thanks. I have to call that detective anyway."

She hung up quickly before Robert could object and dialed the police station.

"Pete Peterson here," the detective answered.

"Detective Peterson, Marge Christensen here," Marge said once she recovered from her surprise at getting through to the detective directly. "I called to ask if you have my husband's car keys or if you know where they might be."

"Call me Pete, please," came the automatic response. "No, we don't have the keys."

Her flash of anger was beginning to feel like part of the normal conversation with Detective Peterson. "You can say that definitively, without checking?" A sigh on the other end of the line only aggravated her more.

"Mrs. Christensen, we don't have so many suspicious deaths in Bellevue that I'm likely to forget the details of any of them. The keys were dusted for prints and left at your house. The only fingerprints, by the way, were your husband's."

Marge was too angry to think about what else she should be telling the detective. With a curt "thank you" she hung up.

While she was still steaming from the conversation, Lori phoned from her office. "Frank called me at work this morning. I wasn't at my desk, so he left a message saying he's going to be out of the hotel for a couple of days. Supposedly a client has invited him to a lake cabin or something. I don't know when I'll be able to talk with him." Her voice shook. "I wish I could get someone to find out what he is really doing. Are you sure I shouldn't call Charles? If he is filing for divorce I want to know about it."

"Yes, I'm sure," Marge insisted. "I guess I'd better tell you why. Charles Froyell was Gene's attorney also. While nothing directly points to him, it's possible he could be the one who talked the men out of the money, maybe even the one who killed Gene."

She heard a gasp at the other end of the line. "Of course I'll wait. I wonder if there is any way I can find out what Frank did with the money while I'm waiting."

"Do you have separate bank accounts?"

"Yes, we do."

"Do you have access to Frank's account?"

"Yes, we have access to each other's accounts."

"Why don't you see if he deposited the money in his account? If he did, find out if it is still there or if he wrote a check."

"Of course," Lori finished. "And if he wrote a check, who it was written to. I'll call the bank immediately."

Marge was relieved to hear a note of energy return to Lori's voice. She could understand. She would feel better once she found a concrete way to solve her own problems.

Before Marge could decide what to do next, Melissa called. "Another Realtor would like to show your house in a half hour. Will that be possible?"

The BMW was bad enough. She hadn't realized how disrupting it was going to be having people trek through the house every day. "Yes, I guess so. I need to go to the grocery store anyway."

At the store, Marge selected Alaska King salmon, asparagus, sourdough bread, and salad makings for their last family dinner in the house. She deserved to splurge after selling the BMW. By the time she returned home, there were no cars that could be the Realtor's or his client's.

Pulling the Honda into the garage, Marge grabbed a bag of groceries and entered through the kitchen door, then stopped short. *Were those footsteps? Was the Realtor still here after all?* Without thinking, she dropped the bag on the kitchen counter and stepped to the doorway leading to the hallway. She peered around the corner only to hear the front door slam.

Marge ran to the front door, grabbed an umbrella on the way, and raced out to the driveway. No one was there. Willy spotted her and came running from his yard.

"What's the problem, Margy?"

"Someone was in the house," she gasped. "He ran out the front door as I came in through the garage. How could he have disappeared so fast?"

Willy looked around and Marge followed suit. They both stopped when they noticed the open garage door.

"I didn't close the kitchen door," she whispered.

"You stay here," he cautioned in a low voice, taking the umbrella from her hand. "He may be hiding in there." With a step surprisingly quiet for one so solidly built, Willy crept toward the garage and disappeared inside. A few minutes later he reappeared through the front door.

"No one here," he said, "But the slider to the deck is open. Did you leave it that way?"

"No, I never leave it open. But, I suppose the Realtor might have," Marge said.

"Realtors are usually careful about things like that. I'd guess your intruder came out the front door, doubled back through the garage, and made his escape through the slider while we were out here. Do you want me to call the police?"

Marge sighed. The kids were due any minute. She didn't want them clucking over her and deciding it wasn't safe for her to stay in her own home. She had too much to do, and she needed her independence to do it.

"No, thanks. I'll check to see if anything is missing. If not, I'll tell Detective Peterson when I talk to him again."

Willy looked skeptical but didn't argue. He returned Marge's umbrella and retreated to his own house.

Marge barely had time to stow the groceries before Kate arrived. "Mom, the house looks great," she declared. "It always looks good, but you've made it more polished than ever."

"From your mouth to the buyer's ears," Marge laughed. "I may have my hopes pinned too high, but Melissa thinks it should sell quickly."

"It will be so strange," Kate said wistfully. She stood at the door to the dining room and gazed at the huge empty desk. "It will really feel like Dad is gone then," she said.

Marge wanted to put her arms around Kate and protect her against the pain of her loss. Was she going too fast, as Gene often claimed she did? Would the children understand the need for her actions?

Kate glanced at her. As if reading Marge's thoughts, she pulled her into a quick hug. "Oh, it's all right, Mom. One of the things I remember you saying so often is 'Life must go on.' You still have yours to live."

Marge returned the hug. How had she ever been blessed with such a daughter? Tears were pricking the backs of her eyelids when the doorbell rang. Marge opened it to admit Caroline and Robert.

Caroline breezed in, almost touching Marge's cheek with a peck, and greeted Kate with a more cordial hug. At least the antagonism of the last meeting seemed to be gone.

They strolled through the house together. Robert found a favorite poster from a basketball game he and his father had attended, which Caroline agreed could go in the room he would eventually have for an office.

"You got the drawer unstuck," Robert exclaimed when it opened easily with his tug.

"Yes, I did," Marge said without elaboration. No need to listen to Robert warning her off again. While the drawer was open, she noticed that the papers were still in place.

Caroline surprised Marge by asking for a decorative mirror from the guest room. Kate ran her hand lovingly over the canopy bed her father had chosen for her, but decided it was too childish for a grown woman. She settled for a side chair, an end table, and one of the bookshelves from the dining room office.

They had stepped into Marge's bedroom to look at a painting Kate thought she might want when Caroline spotted the sketch of Gene that Marge had propped on the dresser.

"This is good," she said. "I'm surprised you never did anything with your artistic talent."

Somehow, coming from Caroline, it felt like criticism. Marge waited until she could be sure her voice was under control before answering.

"I played around with it for a while, when the kids were little, but finally decided I didn't have enough talent or perseverance to make the big time."

"But you did this recently. You haven't lost your edge. There must be many ways to use this kind of talent without making the big time. Have you thought of giving lessons?"

Marge wasn't sure how to answer Caroline. She had given art lessons on a voluntary basis, but never thought of doing it for payment. She didn't think she could charge much, but perhaps it would be enough to make her money last longer while she decided on something more suitable.

"He did look that way, sort of distracted, the last couple of weeks, didn't he?" Kate said, breaking the silence. "I wonder why none of us saw it?"

A familiar pang of guilt shot through Marge. She had obviously seen it, or she couldn't have drawn it. But it hadn't made enough of an impact to get through her self-absorption at the time.

When they returned to the foyer, Robert opened the hall closet to hang his sweater.

"Wow. You sure got Dad's stuff out of the closets fast," he said, accusation in his voice. Kate looked ready to retort, but Marge stopped her.

"I had to look through everything anyway. As long as I needed to clear things out for showing the house, I decided to accomplish both tasks at the same time. It doesn't get any easier if you put it off."

"What do you mean you had to look through everything?" Robert asked.

"I was looking for some clue as to what your father did before he died, and what he could have done with our investment money. I did find some telephone numbers and names here and there."

"Did you learn anything from them?" Kate asked.

"Yes. That he had been in touch with employment agencies and he also commissioned an investigation of some company. I'm waiting for a copy of the investigator's report. I wasn't able to locate the original they sent to your father."

"You have been busy," Kate said, admiration in her voice. "That report could explain a lot about what happened—and why. I think you should go to the police with it as soon as you get it."

"What will it prove?" Robert asked. "Even if it shows Dad lost the money in an investment scam, it won't prove he didn't commit suicide."

"No," Marge said, "but it might lead me closer to whoever did this to him. I've already been in touch with the police, for all the good it did me. And I'll keep bugging them every time I get more information, until they get busy and find out who killed Gene. Which reminds me, one of the reasons I wanted you to come over tonight was to listen to this message I found on your father's answering machine. The voice sounds familiar to me, but I can't place it."

She played the tape several times. Both Robert and Kate shook their heads.

"I agree it sounds familiar," Kate said. "Maybe it's someone who doesn't normally talk so forcefully around us."

Sounding as casual as she could, Marge asked, "Do you know anyone whose initials are NB?"

They all shook their heads.

"Why?" Robert asked, sounding suspicious.

"Oh, nothing. Just a little note I found," Marge hedged.

Caroline spoke for the first time. "You are putting yourself at risk, Marge. If someone has something to hide and they've already killed to hide it . . ."

"Caroline," Robert exclaimed. "Don't encourage Mother in her fantasy that there is a killer out there . . ."

"No, Robert, Caroline's probably right," Kate said. "Mom, you have to promise to go to the police with this. Coupled with the investigator's report, it should be enough for them to at least look into the possibility of fraud, even if they won't change their minds about Dad's death. Just don't take any chances, please. I couldn't bear to lose you, too."

"If you haven't found those keys yet, you should get the locks changed," Caroline said.

"I promise," Marge said, shaken that she had so easily dismissed the missing keys. As usual, she had charged ahead without thinking things through. And Caroline was the only one who saw what she had missed.

Whoever did this couldn't know she was looking into it, could they? As far as the public is concerned, Gene's death was a closed book. So, who had been in the house today? And, if Lori and the children thought the voice on the phone sounded familiar, it must be someone close to them. But, none of them knew an NB. Neither Bruce nor Charles seemed to fit the clues Marge was finding, but they were the only ones close enough to the family, and to Gene's business, to have done whatever had been done.

Dinner proceeded on a lighter note. By the time they ate, it was getting dark and a little chilly; but with the grill close to the house on the deck, they managed the first family meal filled with laughter since Gene's death. It also stirred up memories of other cookouts, successful and disastrous, which brought a few tears. Would it be the same in a different home? Not this house or backyard? It had to be, Marge thought. This was too good to lose.

While they were cleaning up after the meal, Caroline found a private moment to speak to Marge. "I want to apologize for the things I said the other day. Robert's harebrained idea was the last straw at a tense time in our lives. I know I can't blame all Robert's faults on you."

Caroline didn't sound too convinced about that last part, but Marge welcomed the gesture of reconciliation.

"Well, maybe only *some* of them," she said as lightly as she could manage. "The others came out of the box when he was born." She had to bite her tongue to keep from asking if all the faults were Robert's, and if Caroline was blind to any good in him. If this was how she felt, what was their marriage all about?

By the time everyone left it was too late to call the police.

In the middle of the night Marge remembered the missing keys. *Could the killer have them?* Was that how the intruder got into the house? But no, they were still in the ignition of the car when she found Gene. They must be around someplace. The Realtor must have left a door open.

CHAPTER 10

MARGE EMERGED FROM a deep, suffocating sleep. She grappled with the alarm clock, but that didn't stop the noise that had awakened her. She opened one eye. Six o'clock. The realization that she hadn't set the alarm came simultaneously with the knowledge that the intrusive noise was the telephone. She grabbed it seconds before the call went to the recorder, visions of Kate or Robert stretched out in a hospital bed flashing through her mind.

"Mrs. Christensen, are you able to work today?"

"Work? Today?" Marge shook her head. What was the woman talking about? "What work?"

"A small company near Factoria Mall needs someone to cover the phones and do light clerical work for the rest of the week, while the receptionist is ill. It pays six dollars an hour. The hours are eight to five with an hour for lunch."

As the voice droned on it finally penetrated. It was the temporary agency she had signed up with, and promptly forgotten about.

She wasn't prepared.

She had to start sometime.

Marge's voice came out small, uncertain. "Yes, I guess I can do it."

"Do you have paper and pencil handy?"

Once Marge had written down the address and a name to report to and fumbled with hanging up the phone she couldn't think of what to do next. Walking to the window, then to the bathroom, she picked up her toothbrush and started brushing with vigor.

After showering and trying on three different outfits, Marge settled for a lightweight wool-blend suit in forest green that had been one of her mainstays when she did office work as a volunteer. Looking in the mirror, she remembered why it had always been a favorite. It set off her green eyes and auburn hair and made her fair creamy skin stand out. If only she could erase those silly freckles.

Before leaving, she managed to recollect herself enough to get the bed made and straighten up the house in case of a showing while she was gone.

The job was with a small distributor that provided paper products to local fast-food restaurants. Marge quickly learned the names of the three people who worked in the office and how to manage the phones and the coffeemaker. By midmorning she had fallen into a routine of taking the phone orders, filling them out, disbursing, and filing the order forms. She found a few minutes to put in a call to Lori.

"What did you find out?" Marge asked as soon as Lori came on the line.

Lori's voice sounded bright and confident, almost normal. "Frank did put the money in his account. Then he reinvested it. The check was made out to the Cheltington Investment Company. Maybe he isn't leaving me after all."

"Probably not. But the Cheltington Investment Company is the one that endorsed Gene's checks, so it looks like Frank might have made the same investment. You have to find out who made it for him and if the investment was actually made. It might be safer for Frank if you could find out before he comes home."

"You really think his life is in danger?"

"Why don't you look tonight and see if you can find a statement that shows the investment was made? Gene's money has disappeared and that's the only reason I can think of for someone killing him. Even if Frank's money didn't disappear, he can tell us who the Cheltington Investment Company is. If knowing who runs the company means knowing who killed Gene, then Frank could be seen as a threat."

Frightened, Lori promised to look when she got home.

Before breaking for lunch, Marge phoned a locksmith to replace the locks on her house. When she told him about the missing keys, he promised to be there when she returned from work to do the job.

After going to a park near the office to eat the sandwich she had packed, Marge drove to the bank to deposit David's check. At the account manager's suggestion she put half of it in a six-month CD to gain more interest. As long as she was there, she decided to fill out the papers to roll over Gene's IRA into hers. She would drop by the next day to provide a copy of Gene's death certificate. She certainly hadn't needed a lawyer for that.

Marge found the locksmith waiting for her, as promised,

when she arrived home at five-thirty. While he worked she checked the messages. Several people were interested in looking at the desk. She called them back to set appointments for Thursday night.

When the locksmith was finished, Marge changed clothes and ran across the street to Lori's house.

"Have you had a chance to look?" she asked as soon as Lori answered the door.

"Yes, they were buried under a pile of things Frank hasn't handled yet. He's usually better organized than this."

"What did he invest in?" Marge asked.

"A limited partnership called Cypress Hills Development Company."

"The same as Gene!" Marge exclaimed, her hopes rising. "But why can't I find the statements for Gene's investment? Did you get a date off the cancelled check?"

"Yes, Frank made out the check a week before Gene died. The investment confirmation slips are dated a few days after Gene died."

Marge narrowed her eyes. "Aren't investment trades usually completed in three business days?"

Lori nodded. "I thought so. Do you think that means something?"

Marge was sure it meant something—she just didn't know what that something might be.

They went into the kitchen where Lori poured them each a glass of wine and began cutting vegetables for a stir-fry. "You'll stay for dinner," she said, as if there could be no argument. Marge was too lost in thought to disagree.

"Does Charles Froyell have anything to do with your investments?" Marge asked.

"No. We don't use Charles for much. He handled our house purchase many years ago, and we used him to do our wills. Not much else. To my knowledge, Frank has never discussed investments with Charles."

"What about Bruce Wilcox? Do you and Frank know him?"

"We've met him a couple of times at your house. I've never seen him other than that—and I don't think Frank has either."

"So, who do we, or at least Gene and Frank, both know that handles investments?"

They drew a blank.

After they ate dinner and cleaned up the kitchen, Marge returned to her house, feeling she was no further ahead than she had been. She saw three Realtors' cards on her kitchen counter and realized they must have come during the day, before she had the locks changed. She phoned Melissa and got her voice mail. Marge thought of leaving a new key with the Watsons, but their house was already dark. Hoping she wasn't taking too big of a risk, Marge left a message that she would leave the key taped to the bottom of her mailbox.

Two more messages had come in for the desk. She handled those, then trudged upstairs to bed, the day's momentum evaporating into the emptiness of the house. She tossed and turned throughout the night and could barely pull herself out of bed in the morning.

Only three of the prospective desk buyers showed up Thursday evening; but the third one declared the desk was exactly what he was looking for, gave her a check, and said he would come by Friday afternoon with a truck and some friends with muscle to pick it up.

The doorbell rang before Marge had time to pick up the telephone to call Lori. She opened it to find Willy and Wilma, offering a plate of gingerbread cookies.

"Come in, come in," Marge said, laughing. "What a lovely treat to celebrate the sale of that monster desk."

Wilma gave her a quick hug. "It is so good to hear you laugh again," she said. "And even better to know that you are going to land on your feet. You've been gone all day the last two days."

"A job, believe it or not. Just a temporary one, with miniscule pay, but a real job nevertheless," Marge said in answer to the unspoken question. She prepared three cups of instant decaf, since that was what the Watsons drank at night and Marge didn't want to risk a repeat of last night's insomnia. She happily sat down to enjoy the cookies.

"I've been curious about that report you were looking for," Willy said. "Did you ever get a copy of it?"

"No," Marge replied. "I took the check to the investigator on Monday. He said it would only take a day to clear. I asked him to phone and tell me when I could pick up the report, but it looks like he mailed it instead. I should get it tomorrow. I'll call him to be sure."

"I see you and Lori are on good terms again," Wilma said. "I suppose you two are back to discussing everything with each other. It must be comforting to have a good friend so near."

Marge looked at her quickly and turned away. Was it her imagination that Wilma was fishing for information about her and Lori? Was she still bitter about what she considered Lori's desertion during Marge's time of need? Or did the neighborhood busybody's keen nose sense that all was not smooth at Lori's house?

"Lori is a good friend," Marge said. "But, she's not as comforting as your presence has been for the last month." She didn't feel free to discuss Lori's problems with anyone, especially the Watsons. They already harbored enough animosity against Lori. Marge hoped she could hide the concern she felt as soon as they mentioned Lori's name. She looked up to find Willy's gaze on her, appraising.

"Oh, dear! Look at what we've done," Wilma said, and Willy looked away. "We've gone and eaten half the cookies I made for you. I'll have to send over another batch."

As soon as they were out the door, Marge phoned Lori to see if she'd heard from Frank yet. Lori's younger son, Mark, answered and told her Lori was at some women's group meeting and wouldn't be home until late.

Marge hung up and finally took herself off to bed. Her eyes were beginning to close when she remembered she had again forgotten to contact the police about the tape, the papers from the desk, and the intruder.

As soon as Marge arrived at work Friday morning, she phoned Glenn Investigations. The cool receptionist told her the report was mailed on Tuesday afternoon. It should have arrived yesterday or today. Marge could only hope it would be in today's mail.

When Marge returned home, there was no report in the mailbox. She did, however, find two Realtors' cards on the kitchen table, so Melissa had evidently found the key.

It felt strange to know people had wandered through the house, touching, opening, looking at, and judging her belongings. She couldn't help but take a quick look around to make sure everything was in order. If an intruder wanted to get in again, what easier way could there be?

There was a message on the answering machine from the investment broker Gene had consulted. He had not been able to find any trace of a Cheltington Investment Company. He suspected it wasn't a real business. Marge took a deep breath, picked up the phone, and dialed.

"Pete Peterson here," the familiar voice answered.

"Who investigates investment scams?"

"Mrs. Christensen? Is this about your husband?"

"Apparently the Cheltington Investment Company doesn't exist. I want an investigation into the loss of my life savings. I also believe that once you investigate this company, you will find my husband's killer."

The line was silent so long Marge feared they had been disconnected. "Would you like to run that by me again?" he finally said.

Marge took another breath and forced herself to slow down. "I've been unable to find any trace of the Cheltington Investment Company, the name that is stamped as the endorsement on Gene's checks. However, I did find out that he invested in a limited partnership called the Cypress Hills Development Company. He evidently found out something was wrong with the investment because he commissioned an investigation of the company. The original report the investigator sent is missing. I've asked for a copy to be mailed to me."

"None of this proves your husband didn't commit suicide," the detective said, his voice sounding tired.

Anger added force to Marge's voice. "A *crime* was committed. Someone stole our money. And, I'm sure whoever it was killed Gene to keep him from talking. Even if you don't believe that, you should investigate what happened to our money. And you should try to find the check Bruce Wilcox wrote to pay Gene when he bought out the business."

"You say your husband commissioned an investigation?"

If you had done your job right you would know that, she thought. "Yes. Someone tricked him out of the money and he was trying to get it back, I think."

"You think. Tell you what. Because I am sorry that you lost your life savings, I'll have a look at that report. Do you have it with you?"

"No. Since the original report disappeared I had to pay to get a copy. The investigator's office said they mailed it Tuesday, but it hasn't arrived yet."

"Give me the name and number of the investigator."

"I paid a thousand dollars for that report. It belongs to me."

"That's a lot of money for someone who is supposed to be broke," the detective said, his voice dry.

"I'd spend every penny I have to find out what happened to Gene," she retorted. Reluctantly, she gave him the address and phone number. "I also found a message on Gene's answering machine. A man was pressuring Gene into making an investment. I believe it could be the person that killed Gene. The voice sounds familiar but I can't figure out who it is. My children and my neighbors don't recognize it either. Maybe you can use some of your police technology to compare it with voices of people we know."

She could hear him sigh at the other end of the line. "You watch too many TV programs," he said. "When we get the report straightened out, I'll come over and listen to the tape. Is there anyone who doesn't know about it yet?"

Marge gasped. He couldn't think Lori, the Watsons, or the children had anything to do with Gene's death. "No one who could have killed Gene has heard the tape," she said.

"Okay, but unless someone recognizes the voice, I don't know how it will help."

"Oh, another thing. Before you come over, can you please check one more time to see if my husband's keys are still in police possession? I've looked everywhere and haven't been able to find them. I had an intruder in the house the other day, so I had the locks changed, but I need the car keys for the BMW."

"An intruder? The other day? We'll definitely talk about that when I see you."

Marge thought she would rather have faced Robert's concern than the detective's ire over not reporting the intruder. When he spoke again, his voice was gentler. "Are you sure you looked everywhere for those keys? Six months after my father died, my mother found his lost checkbook in the back of the silverware drawer, where only she could have put it."

"I never had my hands on those keys," Marge said, stung by the suggestion that she could be so absentminded.

But in her fog after Gene's death she had put the ice-cube trays in the oven. And caught herself putting dirty socks in her lingerie drawer instead of the hamper. Could she have unconsciously hidden Gene's keys somewhere so she wouldn't have to deal with them and then blocked out the fact that she had even touched them?

The young man came to get the desk at six-thirty. Shortly after he left, Melissa phoned to tell Marge an offer had been made on the house. Marge nearly dropped the phone, her head swimming. She told Melissa to come over as soon as she could. Marge sat and rocked while trying to still the erratic beating of her heart.

"As I said, I'm required to present any offer," Melissa said when they were seated at the kitchen table. "It doesn't mean I think you should take it or even make a counter offer."

Marge stared at the one hundred and fifty thousand dollar offer, her head reeling. Had Melissa been that far off in her calculations?

"Do they give any reason for such a low offer?" she asked.

"They said the house probably needs a new roof, and they have to modernize the kitchen, plus some other things. All of which, of course, we factored into the purchase price."

"Are you telling me I don't have to take this offer seriously?"

Melissa grinned. "You catch on quickly."

With a sigh of relief Marge tossed the offer back across the table.

"No. And no counter offer, either," she said. Her heartbeat slowly returned to normal. "If the buyer can't make a serious offer, I don't want to waste my time."

"Good," said Melissa, sliding the paperwork back into her briefcase. "That takes care of business. Now, tell me about this job."

Marge wrinkled her nose. "It's a start," she said. "I'm finished with it though. It was a short assignment. Until I develop some better skills, I guess it's the best I can do."

"It's a real paycheck and real workplace experience," Melissa reminded her. "The rest will come. In the meantime, shall we do something about that empty dining room?"

"How about if we eat something first?" Marge asked.

They settled for sandwiches and iced-tea. After eating, they spent the rest of the evening rearranging furniture to fill the space left by the removal of the desk. With shelving disbursed to other rooms and furniture borrowed from them to fill the empty spots, the dining room ended up lightly but adequately furnished, while the eating area turned into a small sitting/plant room.

By the time the evening was over, Melissa knew as much about Marge's situation as Marge did.

"Are you sure none of your neighbors could be involved in this?"

"I can't imagine they would be. Gene didn't have any business dealings with any of them. Why?"

"It occurred to me that you've been working the last three days. If the report was mailed, someone might have gotten into your mailbox before you came home."

"But the mailbox is locked . . ." Marge paused.

"What?" Melissa asked.

"I'm sure it's nothing. Just that Gene's key chain, the one we can't find, had a mailbox key on it. I didn't think about changing that lock. Still, I'm sure the keys are around here somewhere. I don't know when they could have been taken."

When she closed the door behind Melissa, Marge slumped against the wall. It didn't matter how late it was, the sudden quiet when she found herself alone in the house released the aching loneliness that lurked just beneath the surface. She would have to ask David how one learned to be at peace with being alone.

The next morning Marge rose before seven. She was showered and heading for the closet before she remembered it was Saturday and her job was finished. Coffee in hand, she wandered through the house, trying to jog something loose. Where could the keys be? Where else might Gene have hidden other information that could lead to his killer? Why did he hide any information from her at all?

"Why can't you tell me what to look for or where to look for it?" she asked.

No answer. "You never tell me anything I don't already know," she cried. She stood still and looked around, as if afraid someone had witnessed her foolishness. Of course Gene couldn't tell her something she didn't already know.

He wasn't real—just a manifestation of her need for him. Wasn't he?

As soon as it was late enough to be sure the Watsons were awake, Marge walked across the driveways to tell them about the open house on Sunday.

Wilma's face was flushed when she opened the door. She appeared flustered for a moment and then stepped outside, immediately closing the door behind her. Marge caught a glimpse of half-packed boxes sitting on the floor before the door shut.

"The place is a mess," Wilma explained. "We're getting ready for spring cleaning and we're doing some painting, so I'm packing a few things out of the way and getting rid of some old stuff. I want to start with a blank page, so to speak, this year. Give the place a new look."

"Don't try to do too much yourself," Marge said, concerned because Wilma seemed to be breathing hard. "I came over to let you know I'll be having an open house tomorrow, so cars will be in and out all afternoon. Until about six o'clock."

"What will you do while the house is being shown?" Wilma asked. Marge was surprised no invitation to spend the time with them accompanied the question. But, if they would be painting and the house was a mess, Wilma would not want company.

"I think I'll take the opportunity to look at some rental places, so I'll be ready to move when the house sells."

Charles phoned shortly after Marge returned home.

"Did you receive a call from Gene in April—probably within days of his death?" Marge asked as soon as she heard his voice.

"No. I'll check my records on Monday, but I'm sure I would remember a call that close to his death. Why?"

"I found a to-do list Gene made, evidently after he began to suspect something had gone wrong with the money. Part of the list was checked off, as if he had completed those items. The first one not checked off was to phone you."

"Whoa, Marge. You lost me. Gene suspected something went wrong with the money?"

Marge suddenly remembered she hadn't kept Charles in the loop, so he presumably didn't know about the investment or her investigation of it. Where should she start? How much should she tell him?

Charles broke in. "Tell you what, why don't I pick you up for lunch? Say eleven-thirty? You can bring me up-to-date."

"I can't. I'm expecting Detective Peterson."

"Detective Peterson? Have the police reopened the case?"

"No, but I'm working on it. I think they should at least investigate the disappearance of the money, don't you?"

Did he hesitate just a moment before answering?

"Yes, they certainly should. Even if they did decide that was part of the reason for the suicide, they still should have investigated the loss of the money. And, I'm ashamed I didn't join in your insistence that they keep going. The evidence you've found erases any doubt in my mind that Gene was at least cheated, if not murdered."

"But he didn't talk to you about it?"

"No. Now that you've told me what it's about, I know that conversation never happened. Let me check with some of my connections and see if there is any record of legal action where Cheltington Investment Company is a party. Since no one can find any record of the company, I'm going on the assumption it is a phony corporation to hide the identity of the person who transacted the deal. I certainly wish Gene had confided in me about whatever he was doing."

Marge shrank back against her chair. She wished Gene had confided in her, too. What if he hadn't confided in Charles or her because he knew they had begun to see each other behind his back? She shook herself. It didn't do any good to wonder what-if. The only way she could make it up to Gene was to remove the stigma his supposed suicide attached to his name.

She picked up the phone, dropped it back down, and went across the street to see Lori.

"Have you talked with Frank?"

Lori grinned. "Do come in," she said. The grin disappeared. "Yes, Frank is back at the hotel and I talked with him. But, he won't tell me anything. He says the investment may have been made several days after he wrote the check, that he doesn't see any connection with Gene's death, and he refuses to smear the name of an innocent person."

"Gene told his brother the most innocent people could be the worst crooks," Marge said. "He's got to tell us that name. It's the only clue to what happened to Gene."

Lori was on her way out to do grocery shopping, so Marge returned home. She took a cup of coffee and sat in her rocking chair. Why was Frank being so evasive? If he would only tell Lori who had made the investment . . .

Marge sat up straight. Why *was* Frank being so evasive? Was it possible he had something to do with the missing money? Had he taken it to fund a new life with another woman after all?

No. That was ridiculous. Frank and Lori had been best friends with Gene and herself forever. Frank would never hurt Gene. But, she never thought he would have an affair, either.

And she didn't know for sure he was having one now. Look how suspicious she had been of Gene, without cause.

She shouldn't jump to conclusions. Besides, if Frank took Gene's money to run off with another woman, wouldn't he have kept his own money, too? Unless he felt honor bound to leave something for Lori when he took off. But why make the same investment?

The ringing of the telephone stopped Marge's racing thoughts.

"I know it's sudden, but I am free this afternoon," Melissa said. "Let's grab a bite of lunch and go look at apartments."

"Today? Will they be open? The house isn't even sold yet. I have no idea where to start. I was going to check the paper before the open house tomorrow. And, anyway, Detective Peterson is supposed to come over today."

"You can't sit around all day waiting for the detective. I'll leave him my pager number so he can let you know when he's coming. There are a couple of complexes not too far from you that always have model apartments open. We'll just look at those, so it won't take too long."

"Well, okay, but we'll lunch here. I was just doctoring some soup that we can have with rolls and salad."

Melissa arrived in fifteen minutes.

"You live alone, don't you?" Marge asked her once they were seated at the table.

"Yes," Melissa said. "I tried roommates, but discovered I needed my own space. Probably why I never married, too."

"How do you fill the time, when you're alone?" Marge asked.

"I don't know." Melissa looked surprised. "Weren't you alone a lot after your children were grown?"

Yes," Marge said. "But it was different. I always knew Gene was coming home."

Melissa sat back, silent in concentration. "I don't *think*

about being alone," she said. "I might put on music, cook, read, do aerobics, watch a movie on TV, call my brothers. I might just sit on my deck or meditate. I guess it's my own retreat from the working world. For you, it might take time to adjust from always thinking about someone else."

Marge felt it was like another betrayal of Gene, trying to eradicate him from her life in order to go on living.

The studio apartments Melissa showed Marge gave her claustrophobia. The one-bedroom apartments felt like cracker boxes. Once she saw the rent prices, Marge didn't even want to look at the two-bedroom apartments; but Melissa insisted Marge needed to get familiar with how prices differed by size, neighborhood, and amenities.

"I won't be able to afford anything with decent space, neighborhood, or amenities—even if I find our savings," Marge said. "I'm spoiled. I know I don't need a place as big as my house, but how do I lower my standards so much?"

"Balance neighborhood and apartment size to get the best you can for the money you can afford. Be willing to pay for that something special that makes you feel good, whether it is a pool, a view, being near a park, even a fountain patio," Melissa advised.

"I can afford those things on six dollars an hour?" Marge quipped.

Melissa laughed. "You won't always make six dollars an hour. Even with your lack of experience, I'll bet some temporary jobs pay better than that. And you may eventually decide to make a career for yourself, like selling real estate."

"Caroline thinks I should look for ways to make my artistic talent work for me."

Melissa shot her a sharp look. "Seems like you've made some headway getting acquainted with your daughter-in-law. It also sounds like she has a good head on her shoulders. Maybe you could do art part-time. Like teaching at home in the evening—and still work at a job."

Marge knew she would consider something like that, but first she had to get her life in order.

By the time they returned to the house, the detective still hadn't phoned. Marge poured them each a glass of white wine and led Melissa to the partially protected deck out back, where the end of a long afternoon of sunshine made it feel like summer.

Marge was too tense to sit. Melissa followed her as she stepped down into the backyard and absently checked the azaleas and fuchsias that were beginning to flower. A glint off something in a large planter at the corner of the house caught Marge's attention. She stepped closer and gasped. There were the missing keys—half in and half out of the pot. How did they get there?

As Marge reached out for them Melissa, who had come up behind her, grabbed her arm. "Don't touch them," she said.

Marge jerked her hand back. "Of course, fingerprints." She studied the keys from a safe distance. "They look polished clean, though. They couldn't have been here over a month. They would be coated with soil after the rain we've had."

Marge looked around and lowered her voice. "That means someone put them here. Probably today. Probably while we were out looking at apartments." She ran into the house to phone the police. To her amazement, the desk sergeant put her straight through.

"Pete Peterson here," came the familiar voice.

"This is Marge Christensen. I found the keys."

The line was silent for a moment. "Good. Then they are no longer missing."

"You don't understand. I found them in a planter in the backyard, shiny and clean, like they were just put there."

Another pause. "Okay. Don't touch them. I was about to come over, anyway. I'll be right there."

Marge and Melissa sat on the deck with a clear view of the corner, waiting for Detective Peterson. "I wonder why whoever put them there didn't bury them," Melissa mused. "You might never have found them, and you wouldn't know how long they had been there if you did."

"Maybe we came back too soon and surprised him. Or a neighbor came by. They look like they might have been tossed from a little ways away."

When Marge opened the door to admit Detective Peterson, she discovered she had forgotten how tall and athletic he was. He loomed in the doorway, broad shoulders blocking out the light. Amazing gray eyes peered at her closely when she greeted him. She had a feeling he could learn more about a person with one of those looks than most people could with an hour's worth of conversation.

"You seem a lot better than the last time I saw you," he said, causing heat to rise in Marge's face.

Marge led him to the deck and pointed to the planter. He stared at the pot and the surrounding area a long time before moving down the steps. "That doesn't look like some place you could have put them without realizing it," he said as he slowly approached the pot, keeping his eyes on the ground. "Especially since you are right, they look too clean to have been there more than a day." Finally, he shook his head and stepped over to the pot.

Marge leaned close to Melissa, not wanting to break the

detective's concentration. "Maybe the person didn't want to leave footprints too close to the planter in the wet grass," she whispered. "Those keys were probably tossed from farther away than we thought. There is no reason they had to land in the pot, that could have been happenstance."

The detective looked up at them. "Good thinking," he said. Marge thought his ears must be as sharp as his eyes. If he was so smart, though, why hadn't he been able to see that Gene hadn't killed himself?

Detective Peterson picked up the key chain with a pencil and deposited it in a plastic bag.

"I'll need your fingerprints to compare to any prints we find on these, though I doubt we will find any. Most likely they were left here because someone was finished with them."

"Well, I got my locks changed Monday. But no one knew that except Melissa."

Melissa looked at her. "And everyone in the neighborhood," she said. "The locksmith came in a van with his name on the side, didn't he?"

Marge nodded.

"Or someone might have tried the keys and discovered they no longer worked," the detective said. "Remember, we don't know who this person is. It is probably someone you know, since the keys were in the car when you found your husband and they disappeared later. Be cautious about who you allow in the house when you are alone. Don't leave any keys hanging out in the open on a key rack. And don't let anyone, even your children, have copies of your new keys until we get this figured out. Now, where is the tape you were telling me about?"

It took Marge a moment to realize the detective was finally taking her seriously. She barely responded when Melissa gave a quick wave and a wink and slipped out the door. By the time Marge retrieved the tape and answering machine, the detective was standing over the percolator, staring at it as if his glare could make it start perking.

Marge pushed the button to start the tape, and then turned to make coffee. No sound emerged from the answering machine. She let the tape run while she finished getting the percolator set up. Still nothing. She rewound the tape to the beginning and played through the messages from the doctor's office. They were there, but when she got to the spot where the man's voice should be, it was blank. She looked at the detective, her eyes wide, fighting a defensive feeling.

"The message has been erased."

"Have you been using the machine?"

"Yes."

"Any chance you could have accidentally erased it?"

"None," she said, stung. He never believed her. "I never used that tape."

"And you have no idea whose voice it was?" Detective Peterson asked.

Marge shook her head. "I know I've heard it before. But I have no idea who it is."

Detective Peterson picked up the tape and put it in another plastic bag. "I'll check it for fingerprints, but you probably smudged any that might have been there."

Marge sucked in her breath. How could she have been so careless?

"Don't blame yourself," he said. Marge looked up in surprise at his solicitation. "If someone, probably your mysterious intruder, erased the tape, I'm sure he wiped it clean afterwards. So, if it is clean we'll know that is what happened."

He reached into his inner jacket pocket and pulled out a

folded manila envelope. "I received this from Glenn Investigations. I had to strong-arm Mr. Glenn into going to the office on a Saturday and making what he says is the third copy of it, but I managed to convince him."

Marge's hands shook as she took the envelope and pulled out a sheaf of papers. Tentatively at first, then anxiously, she scanned through the pages. They detailed Cypress Hills Development Company's financial results for the last five years. She wasn't sure she understood it all, but the average dividend was well over the eight percent Gene had written on the papers she found in Robert's desk. Investing in the company could have turned their nest egg into a nice income. She could find nothing negative in the report, either about the ten-year-old company based in Sarasota, Florida, or about its stock transactions.

In fact, she could find nothing a careful search of public records wouldn't have given her. For this she paid a thousand dollars?

Marge scoured through the report to see if she could find who had convinced her normally conservative but terminally ill husband to put their life savings into a relatively risky limited partnership in order to provide for his widow. She might have known it couldn't be that easy. Nothing had been easy since Gene's death.

If this is what Gene did with the money, it didn't matter who actually handled the transaction—she could claim it regardless. So, when did Gene invest?

The last page of the report was a list of names, dates, and what looked like purchase and sales transactions dating from about two years ago to a week before Gene's death. She ran her finger down the list, but she didn't see Gene's name or the Cheltington Investment Company. Frank's name wasn't there either, but the last date on the page was before Frank's investment was finalized.

Marge was stumped. Did Gene buy this stock or not?

"You might ask my neighbor, Frank Knowles, if he knows anything about the Cheltington Investment Company," Marge said. She couldn't afford to worry about angering Frank. "I found out he made the same investment as Gene, and the check was written to and endorsed by the Cheltington Investment Company. But, he won't tell me or his wife who handled the transaction. He says he won't involve an innocent person."

"Is he home now?"

"No, he's on a business trip. Neither Frank's nor Gene's name appears on this list, but Franks' investment was made after the last date noted here."

"Perhaps Knowles took your husband's money and socked it away, along with his own," Detective Peterson said. "Everything seems to point to someone in your neighborhood."

"But Frank's investment was made. Lori, his wife, found the statement, and there wasn't any extra money in it or she would have noticed. Why would he invest his own money and not Gene's?"

"To cover his tracks. It doesn't make much sense, though, that he used the same brokerage name and partnership as your husband. That creates a connection between them."

"I found some papers Gene left in my son's desk. It looks to me like Gene knew something was wrong before he died and was trying to find out what it was."

"All this appears to confirm your idea that the money went astray without your husband's doing," he said. "But, it is still quite likely that when your husband discovered he had lost the money you would need after he was gone, he felt desperate enough to commit suicide."

"Well, thank you for coming over," Marge said, turning and striding towards the door so he wouldn't have the satisfaction of seeing the angry tears on her face.

"Wait a minute," Detective Peterson said. "I want those papers. They might provide a clue to a professional—something that you overlooked."

Marge didn't know what made her more upset, his insistence Gene committed suicide or his condescension when she was the only one who had done anything to solve this case.

"They're upstairs," Marge said. "I'll get them."

"I'd like to see where you found them, too."

What good would that do? Marge wondered as she led him up the stairs and into Robert's room.

"Who knows about these?" he asked after looking at the papers.

"No one except Charles Froyell," she said. "As you see, he was on the to-do list Gene wrote. I called him today to see if Gene had contacted him, but Gene hadn't."

"Not very smart to call him, was it? He could be considered a suspect. Anyone else?"

"Well . . ." It couldn't be. There was no way they could have made the connection, even if it mattered to them, which was ludicrous. But, she had better tell him, anyway. "My neighbors, Willy and Wilma Watson, saw me go out and come back with the papers in my hand."

"Go out where?"

I'll never learn when to keep my mouth shut, Marge thought. "Out to photocopy them. I put another copy in the other room."

The detective grinned, making Marge squirm. He must realize she had photocopied them so he wouldn't take away her only copy. "As it turns out, that probably wasn't a bad idea. If somehow this copy disappeared, you'd have the backup. The Watsons are the elderly couple next door, right? If they saw you, any other neighbor could have seen you. Since you had an intruder, have you checked to be sure the other copy is still here?"

Marge stared at him and ran into her bedroom to check. The papers were still in the drawer where she had put them.

"Do you know where Frank Knowles is supposed to be staying?"

"No, I didn't think to ask," Marge admitted. It couldn't be Frank, she realized with relief. He wasn't home, and whoever was guilty had been in her house on Monday.

"No problem. We'll find him. I wish you had told me sooner."

"Well, if you were ever around when I call . . ." She stopped. That wasn't fair. A policeman couldn't be expected to sit at his desk and wait for calls to come in, no matter how frustrating it was for her. "Anyway, I just found out about Frank. It took Lori a long time to get in touch with him."

Marge watched the detective walk across to Lori's house after he left. What would this do to their friendship? It couldn't be helped. Frank had to tell them who made the investment.

CHAPTER 11

Sunday morning church appeared to be the best escape from the empty house.

The sunny spring weather made Marge long to wear something light and bright—but she feared some members of the congregation still considered her too recently widowed for that.

An old paisley A-line dress that had been relegated to the back of the closet years ago was a compromise. To her surprise, it slipped on easily. She studied the image in the mirror more closely than usual and stepped on the scale. She had, indeed, shed a few more pounds.

The pleasure of this discovery lifted Marge's spirits and brought a smile to her lips. It disappeared just as quickly. How could she feel such face-lifting emotion with Gene gone? She hadn't even found out who killed him. Still, she couldn't help the slight jauntiness in her step as she walked to the Honda, the skirt swinging just below her knees.

The Watsons' housecleaning was obvious by the pile of trash bags that accompanied their garbage can beside the driveway. Marge wished they had waited until after the open house to put them out.

After the service and coffee hour, Marge stopped to purchase a bunch of flowers to brighten up the house. It was almost noon by the time she returned home. She had entered the house and turned to close the door before she noticed Frank's car in the driveway across the street.

She forced herself to stay in the house. Could she intrude on them today? They had enough problems of their own to sort out without adding hers. But, her problems could well be their problems, too.

Before Marge could decide what to do, Melissa arrived. Marge waited until Melissa was set up and had a fresh pot of coffee perking, then she drove the Honda across the street in order to free up her driveway for house hunters. She parked it in Lori's driveway, next to Frank's car.

The front door of the house swung open before she could knock.

"What did you tell the police about Frank?" Lori demanded.

"So many things have happened. Detective Peterson is finally investigating the loss of our money. All I told him was that Frank also recently invested a large amount of money and it might be through the same company."

"What things?" Lori still blocked the doorway, though her voice was calmer.

Marge stood on the porch while she filled Lori in on the investigator's report, the papers she found in Robert's desk, the answering machine tape being erased, and the keys suddenly showing up.

"Wow," Lori said, finally turning and leading Marge

into the kitchen. "I mean, WOW! I can see why the police are finally taking it seriously."

"Yes, they are. And you need to take it seriously, too. Did Frank tell you anything?"

Lori nodded. Her voice wavered when she answered, "The police made him come home, you know. He was upset and blames you because they seem to think he might have something to do with your money. He just arrived a little while ago and was so tired I let him go to the bedroom to sleep. I did ask him about the money, though. He said Charles has nothing to do with our money or investments. Frank cashed them out himself to take advantage of a good investment opportunity."

"I'm glad to hear about Charles; but I wish Frank had given you the name of the person who did the investing. Has he talked to the police?"

Lori shook her head and made a choking sound. Marge looked at her friend, ashamed of her own thoughtlessness when she saw Lori's eyes rimmed with red and awash with tears. "What, Lori? What is it?"

"I couldn't hold out any longer. I asked Frank if he was having an affair."

Marge grabbed Lori's hands and held them tightly, as if to keep Lori from sinking. She struggled to push her need to know about Gene and the money aside for the moment. "What did he say?"

Lori had difficulty speaking through the tears. "He looked so crestfallen, like a little boy with his hand caught in the cookie jar. He admitted it, Marge. He is having an affair. How could he do this to me?"

"Oh, Lori. I'm so sorry."

It wasn't adequate and Marge could hardly blame Lori if

her main concern wasn't the money. But Marge needed answers. "Lori, the police want to talk with Frank about the investment. Until they can sort out who did what, Frank's life may be in jeopardy. I know it's hard for you, but he has to tell the police who made the investment for him—before someone tries to make sure he never does."

Lori hesitated before going to the bedroom. She came back with Frank trailing behind her. His six-foot-two frame was topped by light brown tousled hair. His gray-blue eyes threw a look of irritation at Marge before they pleaded for understanding from Lori.

What a chameleon, Marge thought. Frank was always the life of the party, able to take on different personalities when telling stories and making jokes. She never considered he might use this talent to his own advantage in this way.

"Please tell us about the change you made in our investments," Lori said, the firmness in her voice surprising Marge.

Frank threw another venomous glance at Marge before responding. "I did invest in Cypress Hills Development, as you know," he said, his voice gruff from sleep. His long legs, which made him look like a gangling youth from behind, carried him to the den and back in a few strides. "Here is the confirmation Lori says she showed you. So, what's the problem?"

"It can hardly be a coincidence that you and Gene both invested in the same company, using the same investment firm. Why would your money get invested and not Gene's?" The words were hardly out of Marge's mouth before a possible answer came to her. "To keep you from getting suspicious and stirring things up right after Gene's death, maybe? Frank, who did this investment for you?"

Frank glared at her. "I don't see how that's any of your

business. I don't agree that it's connected in any way with Gene's *suicide*, and I refuse to drag an innocent person through the mud because you can't accept what happened."

Marge could only stare back. This was a stranger standing before her. Of course, it would take someone other than the Frank she thought she knew to cheat on Lori. "You know Gene's checks were endorsed by Cheltington Investment Company, don't you?"

Frank's head snapped. His eyes were thoughtful, appraising. Finally, he reached a long arm over and snagged his car keys off the key holder on the wall. "I think I'll go talk to the police," he said and loped out of the house.

Lori's voice was almost a whisper. "I forgot to tell him that." After a few moments of stunned silence, she added, "I guess since he left the certificate in the house he didn't plan to leave me, even though he is having an affair." She sounded apologetic at returning to her own worries.

Marge sighed. Maybe the police would have better luck with him. She turned her attention back to Lori.

"Marge, Frank says the affair is over. He wants to come back home and go on with life as if it never happened. But, I don't know if I can trust him. What should I do?"

"Do you still love him?" was all Marge could manage.

"I think so," Lori said. "I miss him. I miss what we had. But I don't know if we can ever have that again."

"Do you think you need some counseling to help you through this? I'm sure I would," Marge offered.

Lori's bark of laughter was more like a catch in the throat. "I doubt you would," she said. "Look at how you've dealt with Gene's death, going after the killer and all. I'd be drowning in misery."

Marge shook her head. "No, I don't think so. When something is final, you might wallow in misery for a while and beat yourself up about it off and on forever, but you pick yourself up and go on. You know you have to.

"The difference for you is that nothing is final. Your mind is telling you it could happen again, no matter what Frank says. I don't think I could deal with that without help. I think if I were you, I'd find a good marriage counselor, and I'd insist Frank go, too, as a condition of coming back home. If your marriage has been anywhere near as good as it seemed from the outside, it is worth the effort to try and save it."

However, when Marge remembered the ease with which Frank slipped in and out of his loving husband persona, she wondered whether it really was worth the effort. And whether the stock purchase might not be one big ruse to throw people off. Had he really gone to the police? She called the station, but neither Frank nor Detective Peterson was there.

"Please let Detective Peterson know that Frank Knowles is in town. He left the house saying he was going to the police station."

There was nothing more they could do, so they nibbled as much as they could of the salad Lori prepared. Fretting about where Frank was and what he was up to, Marge sat in an easy chair. Before she knew it, her pace from the last week caught up with her. She dozed off while Lori was cleaning the kitchen.

Lori woke her after what seemed like only a few minutes, though a glance at her watch told Marge it was nearly five o'clock.

"Phone call," Lori said. "It's the detective. Your Realtor told him you were here."

"Mrs. Christensen, this is Pete Peterson."

"Yes?"

"I wanted to let you know the keys and the tape recorder were wiped clean of fingerprints, so there's no need for you to be printed at this time. And, while the money and your husband's death aren't necessarily connected, the fact that someone went to so much effort makes me wonder if someone also went to a great deal of trouble to make your husband's death look like suicide. So, while we still have no indication his death was anything other than suicide, I thought you would like to know I am reopening the case."

"Thank you," Marge choked out. The two words, all she could manage, were hardly adequate for the gratitude that brought a lump to her throat. "Is Frank Knowles there with you?"

"No. I was going to ask you where he was."

"He left here before two saying he was going to the police," Marge explained. "He wouldn't tell us who had made the investment for him."

"I'll put out an APB to find him. If your suspicions are correct and he isn't guilty himself, his life may be in danger."

By the time Marge hung up the phone, she was wide awake. After telling Lori what the detective had said, she tried to steer the conversation clear of Gene or Frank while they waited for the open house to end. When the driveway emptied shortly before six, Marge took a chance and returned home. The pile of trash for Monday's garbage pickup had grown on the Watsons' side of the driveway. Marge grinned at her mental picture of Wilma showing off her newly cleaned and decorated house.

Melissa ran out to retrieve the open house sign and put it in the trunk of her car before joining Marge.

"So," Marge asked. "What's the story?"

"I think we have an offer coming," Melissa said, her eyes

shining. "The buyers came with their own agent, so they are now talking it over and working out what they want to do."

Marge tensed against the speed with which her life was changing. If this was right for her, shouldn't she feel at least some of the excitement she saw in Melissa's face?

"When do you think the offer might come?"

"If they make an offer it will probably be by tomorrow night. It could come in today, but I'd be surprised."

"Wow," Marge said, sitting down hard. "I mean, Wow! I don't know whether to hope it does or it doesn't."

"What you need to do is stop thinking about something that hasn't happened yet," Melissa said. "How was your afternoon? I see you ended up across the street. Isn't that the neighbor you wanted to talk with?"

Marge filled her in. "I can only hope Frank really did go to the police."

After Melissa left, Marge was so tired she couldn't manage more than canned tomato soup doctored with frozen peas, carrots, and leftover rice for dinner. She called both Kate and Robert to bring them up-to-date.

Kate said she was relieved to know the police were back on the case. "I've looked into those records on the business and talked with people who know how it works. The records show Dad was still a partner in the business. Bruce added another partner but never bought out Dad."

"But I saw the receipt," Marge protested. As far as she knew, Frank didn't even know Bruce, so how could Bruce have made his investment? Bruce hadn't been in the house since before Gene died, so he couldn't be the one who got the keys. The pieces still weren't fitting together.

"That's something we'd better tell the police. Once they decided it was suicide, I don't think they looked at anything very closely. I don't know what this means, except the paper-work didn't get done, but they need to check all the angles."

Robert was also relieved to learn that the police were investigating. "You can leave it to them and be out of danger," he said. Sure, Marge thought when she sat in her rocking chair, leaned back, and closed her eyes. Like every-one left it to the police before. Well, it was too late to worry the police about Bruce tonight. If he had cheated her, he thought he got away with it so he wasn't going anywhere before she had a chance to talk with Detective Peterson in the morning. But she was almost positive it wasn't Bruce's voice on the tape urging Gene to make the investment.

What more could she do to find Gene's killer? Since Detective Peterson was back on the case, she knew he would agree with Robert that she should stay out of it. But if she had done what Peterson wanted, he wouldn't be back on the case. Robert couldn't seriously think she was going to qui-etly wait to see if the police could solve it this time.

"Not likely."

Marge jumped and quickly looked around.

"So, you were going to make this great investment that would take care of me after you were gone," she responded, hoping to entice Gene's voice into talking more, maybe giving her a clue. "You gave the money to someone to make the investment. But, you didn't get confirmation of the investment, so you got worried. You made the checklist as a plan of action to find out what happened. When you got the investigator's report you found out you weren't listed as a stockholder, and you should have been."

"You always could solve a puzzle when you put your mind to it," Gene's voice said.

But the puzzle wasn't solved yet and the voice wasn't

forthcoming with more information. Marge went upstairs to get her copy of Gene's list. She stared at it, hoping if she concentrated hard enough she could figure it out.

1. Check with broker ✔
2. Bank for cancelled check ✔
3. Confront Nb ✔
4. Get independent report on Cypress Hills ✔
5. Confront Nb again?
6. Call Charles Froyell
7. Lawsuit ????
8. Police ????

Who was Nb? It must be the person who made the investment. "Oh, Gene, why did you have to be so obscure? No one else would see the list unless something happened to you. You didn't need to hide it so thoroughly and mask the identity of the thief so completely."

But that was exactly what he had to do. Gene always bent over backwards to be fair. And this time he had bent over so far it had killed him.

Marge had to clear her head, to think about something else for a while. Only one thing would work. She picked up her sketchpad, sat with the pencil hovering over it for a minute, and closed her eyes. Almost before she re-opened them, the pencil started to move. She smiled as she drew. *Wilma's redecorating must be on her mind.* The figures that appeared were Willy and Wilma proffering a plate of gingerbread cookies.

As Marge put the final touches on the sketch, her mind wandered back to the list Gene had made. After he had the copy of the cancelled check, his next step was to talk to the mysterious Nb a second time. If he had, it was probably the last thing he ever did. Since that was the first item not checked off his list, he evidently didn't get to the rest.

"The most innocent-seeming people were sometimes the most crooked," Gene had told Larry.

Okay, so who were the most innocent-seeming people among those close enough to do what they had evidently done? Who would she never consider, even if someone mentioned their names? Who was she the least inclined to suspect? Frank and Lori? Could be.

No.

She looked again at the picture in front of her. *The most innocent. With the most opportunity.* A chill of disbelief crept up her back.

She did suspect Frank, so he wasn't the least likely.

She suspected Bruce, so he wasn't the least likely.

She suspected Charles, so he wasn't the least likely.

Marge shook her head. It couldn't be the only people she would never suspect. She looked at the list again. Nb. How did that tie in?

Suddenly she jumped out of the chair, sending it crashing to the floor behind her, ignoring the scream of pain that shot through her leg muscles. "Oh, my God! Gene! You made it so obvious. How could I have missed it?" she cried. She ran for the telephone and dialed the police station.

"Detective Peterson, please," she said.

"I'm sorry, he's not available. Can someone else help?"

"I know it's late, but it is important that I get in touch with him. Doesn't he have a cell phone or something?"

"Please give me your message and I'll see that he gets it."

Marge was ready to scream, but it seemed she had no choice. "Please ask him to call Marge Christensen immediately. I believe I know who killed my husband."

She hung up the phone and went to peer out the

window. Everything looked normal. She could see flashes of light through their living room window, like the changing screen of the television. She looked at the clock.

Only eight o'clock. Time seemed to drag on interminably. How could she possibly wait for Detective Peterson's call?

Marge peeked out the window again. Everything looked the same. Exactly the same. She stared for a while and saw no hint of movement in the house; nothing except the flashing light from the television.

She couldn't wait any longer. Not after seeing all the trash on the curb and the boxes stacked in the house. She slipped out the back door and walked quietly across the back lawn, where she wouldn't be visible in the dark. Once she reached the Watsons' house, Marge crouched and made her way to the living room window. She lifted her head up high enough to look inside.

No one was there. No boxes on the floor. Just the TV showing one of those gross reality shows—the kind Wilma and Willy never watched.

Marge stood straight and hurried to the garage door, trying to peer through the high window—but it was too dark inside to see whether a car was there or not. As she turned back towards the living room window she saw that the pile of trash bags awaiting the early Monday morning pickup had grown even larger since she had returned to her house. Did the Watsons accidentally leave the television on while they worked in the back of the house?

Marge stood at the living room window and peered closely, certain that no one was going to see her. She almost missed the movement through the open door of the den, barely visible from where she stood. She heard a crash and saw a chair with someone in it fall into the doorway.

It was Frank.

Tied and gagged.

Before she could react, the detective's car pulled into her driveway.

"It's Frank Knowles," she cried. "He's tied up in the Watsons' house. They must be the ones who took our money. Frank must have gone to talk with them before going to the police. They're gone. You have to stop them."

Detective Peterson stared her into silence. He turned to look through the window before going to his car and talking into the radiophone.

"Okay," he said when he finally returned. "I have help coming, with authorization to enter the house." Marge was surprised at how calm she had become. "Do tell me, though, how you came to the conclusion these neighbors you were so sure were innocent a short time ago are now the guilty ones."

Marge fidgeted, sensing the Watsons getting farther away while they stood and talked. But, she knew she couldn't hurry this detective. "First, Gene told his brother, Larry, that it was the most innocent-seeming people who were often the worst crooks. The most innocent people we know are Willy and Wilma Watson."

"Hardly damning evidence," the detective said dryly.

"And the list," Marge continued, as if he hadn't spoken. "The first item not checked off on the list was Nb. Nb for neighbor."

"So far, in addition to the Watsons, you've described Frank Knowles and everyone else who lives on this block."

Frustration jumbled Marge's thoughts. "Don't you see Frank in there? He left his house hours ago, saying he was going to talk to the police. He told us everything except the name of the person who handled the investment. The only reason he would have for coming here would be to confront

Willy Watson, and he probably found them in the process of leaving."

"If it makes you feel any better, we have been checking on all your neighbors. It is suspicious that we haven't found any history on the Watsons before they moved to Bellevue six years ago. And, of course, Frank Knowles' plight in there seems to put the cap on it. But, so far, there is no proof they took your husband's money, and certainly no proof they killed him."

Marge couldn't stand it any longer. "The Watsons are probably getting away while we stand here talking. Isn't there anything you can do?"

The detective smiled. "I'm not quite that dense, Mrs. Christensen. I have men checking the airport, bus station, and train station as we stand here. It will be hard for them to slip past."

"How do they know what the Watsons look like?"

"I gave them a description. It would be better if they had a picture, though. Do you have one available?" He included Lori, who had walked up to them, in the question.

"Oh, Marge. I'm so sorry I didn't insist Frank tell me," she said. "I saw the Watsons pull their car out of the garage almost an hour ago. It seemed strange to see them go out so late on a Sunday, but I had no reason to be suspicious."

"An hour!" Marge turned to Detective Peterson. "They could have disappeared already! What are you doing here?"

While Marge was berating Detective Peterson, the police arrived and entered the house. A short while later an officer came out and spoke to the detective. "The house is clean as a whistle," he said. "The victim is all right. He said to tell you that it was Willy Watson who made the investments. These guys must have done this before, because that spring-cleaning completely wiped out any trace of them. No photos, nothing personal, not a fingerprint so far. Even the garage and tool shed have been cleaned out. We'll look through that pile of trash, but they could be long gone before we find anything useful."

Remembering the sketches she had recently finished, Marge ran into her house and returned as the detective was directing a police officer to take Frank to the squad car.

Detective Peterson turned back to Marge and Lori. "The photos?" he asked.

Lori shook her head. "I thought they were camera shy. They always refused to be a part of any group photo."

"I can give you the next best thing," Marge said, holding up the sketches."

"I'm impressed," Detective Peterson said as he took them and sent them off to the police station to be copied and distributed. "Since we haven't found any fingerprints, your drawings could make the difference in identifying them before they can get out of town."

"I can't believe those two," Lori declared. "Spending all that time with you, acting like they cared so much, when they were the ones who killed Gene. They were probably just keeping an eye on you to see if you were getting close to figuring out what really happened."

"Normally, it is out of character for con artists to resort to violence," Detective Peterson cautioned. "They would more likely have tried to talk their way out of any problem. There is still no solid evidence Mr. Christensen didn't commit suicide."

As soon as Detective Peterson drove away, presumably to join the search, Marge turned to Lori and whispered, "Let's go to the airport."

"Are you crazy?" Lori whispered back. "They might not even be using the airport. Or they might have already flown out. Anyway, if they *are* there, the police will be able to spot them from your sketches. I don't think Detective Peterson would be happy to have us interfering."

"I can't stand here and do nothing. I might recognize them before the police do. I'm going. Are you coming with me or are you going to talk with Frank?"

Lori stared for a moment across the street, where Frank peered back from the squad car window.

"I can't face him just yet," she said. "And, I don't owe him anything. Let's go."

Marge went into the house to grab her car keys. They quickly climbed into the Honda, in front of an astonished Frank, and sped away before any of the officers could realize they were leaving and try to stop them.

The stretch of I-405 between Newport Hills and the turnoff for the airport never seemed so long, even though Marge broke all the speed limits getting there. After a frustrating search in the airport garage they finally found a parking spot and raced across the sky-bridge to the main terminal.

"This is crazy," Lori said, eyeing the hordes of people heading in every direction. "We don't even know which terminal they might leave from."

Marge hesitated a moment. "If I were in their shoes, I'd be leaving the country. Let's go to the south satellite. All of the international flights depart from there."

They ran down the escalator, walked sedately through the security gates, and impatiently waited two minutes for the shuttle to the satellite terminal.

While the south satellite was a smaller area, the number of people milling around still made their search a daunting task. "Why must so many flights take off at the same time?" Marge complained. She spotted a couple of policemen moving from gate to gate with her sketch in their hands. She and Lori turned to head in the opposite direction, so the shops and service area in the center of the building blocked them from the policemen's view.

After a complete walk around the area, while averting their faces and endeavoring to look like innocent travelers whenever they crossed paths with the policemen, Lori was ready to give up. "I'm convinced this is crazy," she said. "Even if they are here, they might be disguised. And, if they've seen the policemen or us, they're probably hiding anyway."

Lori might be right, but Marge refused to give up. She needed to face the people who had stolen her savings and probably the last few months of Gene's life, taking away her time to say good-bye to him. Also she wanted to confront the hypocrisy of the Watsons acting as though they cared for her well-being after Gene's death

As Lori and Marge made a second round of the south satellite they stopped conversing, feeling the strain of the evening. Suddenly Marge stopped and stared at a portly couple in line at the gate to board a flight to Amsterdam. She couldn't see their faces. The man had a full head of salt-and-pepper hair. The woman's brown hair was coiled in a soft French twist. There was something about the set of the shoulders . . .

Marge grabbed Lori's hand and motioned her to be quiet. She pulled Lori into the seating area, towards the windows, where they could get a frontal view of the couple. When the woman turned her head, Marge saw wire-rimmed glasses framing brown eyes. *Contacts*, she thought. The lips were drawn into a hard line with bright red lipstick. There seemed to be no trace of Marge's gingerbread-baking neighbor, but the shape of the woman's face and the set of her shoulders weren't so easily disguised. That was all Marge needed to see to make an identification.

Marge looked around frantically. The policemen were nowhere in sight. "Go find the police," she whispered hoarsely to Lori. "I've got to stop them before they get on that plane."

Lori tried to hold Marge back, but Marge ducked out of her grasp and ran towards the couple. Out of the corner of her eye Marge saw Lori take off in the opposite direction.

Willy turned and saw Marge coming. He tried to push his way past the couple in front of him to get into the aircraft entryway, but they pushed back. Marge reached him and, dodging the hands of an airline employee who tried to stop her, grabbed the salt-and-pepper wig and tore it off Willy's head. "Don't let them on the airplane," she cried. "They're not who they say they are."

She managed to get Wilma's wig half off her head before Willy's strong arms encircled her, pinning her arms to her sides. Marge struggled to breathe; feeling bruises form on her arms as Willy squeezed tighter. Wilma turned to the ticket collector, pulling herself up to her full five feet three inches while trying to straighten the brown wig on her gray hair. "Let us on our flight immediately and call security to take charge of this crazy woman!" she demanded.

The ticket collector looked around helplessly. Another airline employee closed the door to the aircraft entryway. Willy turned in a circle, Marge's feet barely skimming the floor as he dragged her with him. Two security guards were approaching, but Lori and the policemen were nowhere in sight.

"Come and take this maniac off my hands," Willy demanded. "She's disrupting the whole flight."

Marge gasped. That was the voice from the tape! No

wonder she didn't recognize it—she had never heard Willy speak like that before. And to think the Watsons were among the first people she had asked to listen to the tape.

The security guards reached out to take Marge, but she kicked out and drove them back. "Get the police," she cried. "They know who these people are. You can't let them board the plane before the police get here."

"That sounds reasonable," one of the guards said. "Why don't we all just sit down and wait for the police? The airplane isn't going anywhere until this is settled."

Willy's grasp loosened. Before Marge had time to react, he threw her at the security guards, grabbed Wilma's hand, and pulled her away from the gate towards the escalator.

"I don't think so," Marge heard Detective Peterson's voice boom out. She looked up to see him approaching from the direction of the escalators, in the center of a team of police officers. Willy turned and started to pull Wilma in the other direction, but Lori and two more policemen greeted them. Finally, he stopped and dropped Wilma's hand.

"I'm sorry, baby," he said. Wilma only glared at him. As the officers handcuffed them, Wilma turned her icy stare on Marge. This was a stranger. There was no trace of Wilma in that look.

Tears prickled Marge's eyes. First she had lost Gene, and now Willy and Wilma. Where was the anger? Where was that desire for revenge that had propelled her to the airport? She sagged. A strong hand reached out to support her.

She looked up to see Detective Peterson's stony eyes. "That was a damned fool thing to do," he said as he led her to a chair. "He could have killed you."

Marge shook her head. "I don't think so. I think they could see it was already hopeless, even though they made that last-ditch effort to get away. And, I don't think they are killers."

"So, are you finally convinced your husband committed suicide?"

"How can you say that?" Lori cried, coming up behind Detective Peterson. "They must have killed Gene. And you said whoever killed Gene might kill Frank, too."

"They probably made the investment for Frank," Marge offered, "to try and put an end to the investigation. If they had killed Frank instead, nothing would have pointed to them."

She turned to the detective. "But, no. I'm still convinced someone killed Gene. I just don't know that it was Willy. Do you think I could talk with them sometime, Detective Peterson? I have something else to tell you, but I need to know what Wilma and Willy say first."

"Call me Pete," he said automatically. "I'll see what I can arrange. Although it will only happen if the Watsons are willing to talk with you."

Eventually they found their way back to the car. Lori drove, since Marge's arms were sore and felt like they were weighted with lead after the abuse from Willy. Once home, Marge managed to pull off her clothes and collapse into her bed. She would rest only a minute before putting some ice packs on her arms.

CHAPTER 12

THE SHRILL OF THE telephone awoke Marge at six the next morning. After two groggy tries, she managed to stretch her arm far enough to lift the receiver.

"We received excellent feedback about your performance last week," the cheerful voice of Linda at the temporary agency said. "I have another job available today, perhaps more than one day."

"Oh, no," Marge groaned, struggling to wake from a deep sleep. Was it possible only two days had gone by since she finished the temporary assignment? Could she refuse an assignment this soon? Could she afford to? She'd have to. She had to talk with Willy. "I'm afraid I won't be able to work today." Marge couldn't think of an adequate excuse, so she didn't try to explain.

"I'm sorry to hear that," Linda said. "Will you be available the rest of the week?"

Marge had no idea. She knew she wouldn't work again until she had all the answers to what had happened to Gene.

"Probably not," she replied.

"Give me a call when you are able to work again," Linda said in a voice that was decidedly less cheery.

Marge was unable to return to sleep and it was too early to contact the police. So, she filled the bathtub with warm water and sank into it for a long soak. The water had completely cooled before she pulled the drain and maneuvered her way out.

By the time she had downed two Tylenol and finished her first cup of coffee, Marge wished she had gone to work. Waiting for the detective to phone and tell her she could talk to the Watsons was nerve-wracking.

She turned the radio volume high and started to pace. When she realized what she was doing she grinned. *This was getting to be habit-forming.* Marge's thoughts flipped back to her neighbors. Something wasn't right. Not in her wildest dreams could she imagine Willy—or Wilma—killing Gene.

She switched off the radio and ran upstairs to get the papers Gene left in Robert's desk. Clearly Gene did two different things with the money. Supposedly their savings went into Cypress Hills Development Company. But, Gene handled the business money separately and she didn't have a clue what he did with it.

She started when the phone rang and jumped up to answer it. It wasn't the detective, it was Melissa. "I'm on my way over," the Realtor said. "And I'm bringing a bottle of wine, in case you feel like celebrating."

Marge swallowed her disappointment and tried to turn her thoughts back to the house. So much had happened since the open house yesterday she had forgotten all about it. She splashed cold water on her face and refreshed the percolator before the doorbell rang.

Marge's throat constricted as she read the purchase agreement, scouring it for a reason not to sign. There wasn't one. The offer was barely lower than the list price, well above what she and Melissa had decided was the least she should consider. The closing date was set for mid-June, giving Marge plenty of time to make other living arrangements.

Marge leaned back and closed her eyes. Everything was happening too fast. She really should have allowed herself time to get used to one change before another came crashing down. But, she needed the money. And, no matter how she felt about it, she didn't need the house.

She quickly signed the agreement.

That done, they went out to the deck, where Melissa opened the wine and poured two glasses. "Congratulations," she said. "You have taken a giant step forward."

Marge took a large gulp and felt the warm smooth liquid slide down her throat. When it hit her empty stomach, its mellowing effect spread fast. She sipped again.

"Everything else I've done so far was easy compared to this," she said. "This will change my life completely."

"It may be coming a little fast, because of the financial necessity," Melissa said, "but it would happen someday anyway. You're too strong a woman to be satisfied living in the past. I already see you reaching out to embrace the future."

Marge stared at her. "Strong woman? Me?"

Melissa laughed. "Look in a mirror sometime. Who has, in less than two weeks, come out of mourning, sold a car and a house, started a job, and tracked down the first leads towards finding her missing money—when even the police couldn't do it? Plus, losing at least one dress size in the process."

Marge couldn't stop herself from laughing with Melissa.

At that moment, Lori came around the corner of the house. Marge introduced her two friends.

"Have you told Melissa about our adventures last night?" Lori asked after informing Marge that she had sent Frank away until she could sort out her feelings.

When Marge admitted that she hadn't, Lori filled Melissa in.

"You did what?" Melissa gasped, her face full of a combination of consternation and admiration. "I just said you were a strong woman. I guess I didn't know the half of it."

Marge could only shrug. In hindsight, she couldn't explain what led her to take such foolhardy action. Fortunately it had succeeded. And, that was all that mattered to her.

"I still can't figure out why they invested the money Frank gave them," Lori said. "If they were going to take off anyway, why didn't they just keep it?"

"Maybe they thought they wouldn't have to leave," Melissa suggested. "The police had determined Gene's death was a suicide. Nothing connected them to the loss of Marge's money. It looked like they were home-free."

Marge suddenly felt too tired to think. Melissa took one look at her and led her into the house, Lori trailing behind. "You sit down in that rocking chair. Lori, I know it's early, but we have enjoyed a glass of wine and it sounds like you could use one, too. Marge has had enough. Time for an early lunch, I think."

While Melissa and Lori concocted a tempting lunch with rice and frozen vegetables and shrimp, they stayed resolutely off the subjects of Gene's death and the theft of the money. Melissa learned about Frank's infidelity. She was less inclined than Marge to think Lori should give him a second chance; but then, Melissa had never experienced years of building a life together with someone.

"I'd be so unhappy without him. Yet, I'm miserable with him," Lori said. She turned to Marge. "How do you manage without Gene?"

Tears came to Marge's eyes. "I stay very busy," she said. "When I stop moving, I get so lonely. I wonder if I'll ever be truly happy again."

Melissa glared at them. "So, you are both telling me that you can't be happy without your husbands? That you have no other source of happiness?"

Lori looked thoughtful. "Well, when the kids . . ."

"But your kids are grown," Melissa said. "Don't you ever feel happy all by yourself, without reference to anyone else?"

"Sometimes," Marge ventured, "when the weather is perfect and the mood is just right."

"Where does that happiness come from?"

Marge and Lori looked at each other.

"Listen up, you guys," Melissa said. "I've been alone most of my adult life. I haven't been miserable. I haven't been lonely. Why? Because my happiness is inside me. If I ever meet Mr. Right, I suspect I'll want to hang onto him forever; but I hope I don't ever depend on him for my happiness." She turned to Lori. "If I were you, I'd be angry at Frank for betraying your trust. I'd be upset that what you had may be gone. But, if you're going to make the right decision about whether to get back together with him, you have to know you can go on and have a fulfilling and happy life without him."

Marge was sure it wasn't that easy, but she hoped Lori would take Melissa's words to heart. Gene was gone. Marge had no choice but to learn to go on without him. Lori had a choice and, if she could internalize Melissa's philosophy, she would be more likely to make the right decision.

Detective Peterson had not called by the time Lori and Melissa left. Marge phoned Kate to let her know the house had sold and that the Watsons had been arrested. Putting it into words made it seem even more unbelievable.

Predictably, Kate moaned a bit about the house. The news about the Watsons was met with stunned silence. "I can't believe it," she said, her voice barely above a whisper. "I feel like I've lost a set of grandparents. I think I need to hang up now to digest this. But Mom, could they really have killed Dad? And, what about Bruce and the money from the business?"

"I don't know," Marge said. "I can't believe they are killers either. But, why would Bruce kill Gene? He has a new partner. All he had to do was buy Gene out. The business is low-budget. It wasn't enough money to kill for."

Marge started to phone Robert, changed her mind, and called Caroline instead.

Caroline sounded startled to hear Marge's voice. "Couldn't you reach Robert?" she asked.

"I didn't try. I wanted to call you for two reasons: to let you know the house has sold and to see how things are going."

"Things are fine," Caroline's cool voice replied, an accent on the first word. "Congratulations on selling the house."

Marge winced, but refused to be put off. "Have you found a place yet?" she asked.

"Yes, we signed an agreement yesterday," Caroline answered. "I thought Robert would have called to tell you."

"That's wonderful," Marge said. She bit back the disappointment that Caroline always left it to Robert to share information with her. Although, she had been doing the same thing. "What's it like?"

Caroline's voice warmed slightly as she described the small condominium on the tip of Lake Washington, with three bedrooms and a sweet little view of the lake framed by trees. "It's practically on the Burke Gilman Walking Trail," she added. "In fact, the first thing I thought when I saw it was that it might be perfect for you. But a little pricey in your current situation, I'm afraid."

"It does sound lovely," Marge answered, surprised and pleased she had come to Caroline's mind in some way. "I'm sorry I never knew you also enjoyed walking and jogging."

"I jog mostly. But, when Robert told me how you like to take long walks, I thought we might share at least one activity." She laughed, sounding embarrassed at the admission. "What about you? Where are you going to live?"

"That's a good question. I've barely begun looking at apartments and I haven't seen anything of interest yet. Will you let Robert know about the house, or shall I call him?"

"I'll tell him. I might also have some ideas about where you should look for an apartment. Thanks for calling me."

Marge stared at the telephone. Had she imagined it or was Caroline's attitude thawing ever so slightly?

She glared at the clock. She wanted to pick up the phone and call the police station. What would she say, though? Detective Peterson promised to let her know if the Watsons were willing to talk with her.

As if responding to her thoughts, the phone rang. Marge sighed with relief when she heard the voice on the other end of the line.

"Mrs. Christensen. Pete Peterson here. Willy Watson has agreed to see you. I hope you can learn something from him because, while we're convinced they took your money, all the evidence we have so far is pretty circumstantial. Willy won't say a word and Wilma categorically denies everything. And she claims to be distraught that you would think such things of them. Wilma is against talking to you, but she insists on being in the room when you talk with Willy. She will be antagonistic."

Marge's heart flipped. *What if she were wrong?* What if she had wrongfully accused her neighbors, especially after they were so good to her? What if they were just off on some kind of fantasy vacation and she needlessly frightened and upset them at the airport?

"Do you think they could be innocent?" she asked in a weak voice.

The detective's laugh was strong, sending reassurance across the telephone line. "After we discovered through the fingerprint trace how many times they've pulled the same scam they did on your husband? And, with Frank Knowles' corroboration that they made the same investment for him, using the same endorsement stamp? Not a chance," he said.

When Marge arrived at the police station she found a different Willy and Wilma. Willy looked sunken and defeated. Wilma glared at Marge with icy blue eyes.

"How could you tell the police you thought we had anything to do with Gene's death?" Wilma demanded as soon as they were alone. "When we did everything we could to be good neighbors to help you? How could you do that to us?"

"Why were you running away?" Marge asked.

"Just because we left without telling you doesn't mean we were running away. Our lives are our own business," Wilma retorted. "Since when is it a crime to take a vacation? Why couldn't you accept what happened, the way the police said it did? Why did you have to go stirring everything up, as if it mattered when he was going to die anyway?"

Marge reeled back as if she had been struck. She couldn't believe this was Wilma talking. How could she say that? How could she feel that way? As if it mattered. Dear God, of course it mattered. Whether weeks or months or years, Gene was robbed, not only of his money, but also of his life. Marge and the kids were robbed, too, not only of their money, but also of Gene's presence. Of the chance to say good-bye. How could it *not* matter?

It almost sounded like Wilma was admitting to murder. "So, you did kill him, after you took the money," Marge suggested.

"Why would we kill Gene? What possible reason could we have?"

For a second Marge couldn't think of one.

"To keep him from turning you in for stealing our money," Marge replied.

"What money? Does it look like we have money? Can you find *your* money anywhere in our possession?"

Willy sat slumped in a chair, shrunken and quiet. Marge gave him a pleading look. She thought he was the one who wanted to talk.

"Why would you clean out the house if you were only going on vacation?"

Wilma sniffed. "I never left a house dirty in my life. I didn't want to leave any of our personal stuff out for thieves to rummage through while we were gone."

Marge shook her head. "Detective Peterson told me they found all your personal belongings packaged and ready for shipping in a storage unit near SeaTac Airport. You were moving and you planned to have someone send them to you later."

Willy finally spoke. "I'm so sorry, Margy. If I'd known he would kill himself . . ."

"Willy, shut up," Wilma interrupted.

"It's no use, Wilma," he said, his voice hoarse. "They've got our fingerprints now."

"Shut up, you old fool," Wilma repeated.

Willy was shaking his head. "All these years, ever since you first made me prove I loved you, I've been doing what you asked me to do. You were everything to me. I couldn't bear to disappoint you." He looked at Marge. "I never killed anyone and I didn't kill Gene. But if he killed himself because of what I did, then it was my fault, just as if I did do it."

"You didn't kill him, Willy. And so what if he killed himself? He was dead anyway."

"How did you do it?" Marge broke in, finding it hard to breathe. "And why?"

Willy stared at Wilma with a beseeching look for so long Marge was afraid he wasn't going to answer. When he did start to speak again his voice sounded old, defeated. "I was a successful stockbroker when I married Wilma. She talked me into this plan to get someone's money, as if to invest it, then we'd keep it and leave with changed identities before anyone could figure out what happened. She had contacts for fake IDs and the cosmetic work we needed in case someone started to look for us too soon. Your detective has probably discovered we did the same thing several times, for more money each time. Every time I thought we were finished, that we had enough . . . Wilma always decided we needed more."

"But you don't live like you have a lot of money," Marge interrupted, puzzled.

"That's right," Wilma declared, triumph in her voice.

"The old fool has gone senile. He's been having these fantasies for years. Why would we live in a dumpy neighborhood like yours? If we had the money he's talking about, we could afford the best."

Willy heaved a huge sigh, as if finally realizing he had no hope of regaining Wilma's affections. "We always spent a lot right after we left a place. We would travel overseas for a while, letting things cool off. Before returning, we went on cruises and lost money in the ships' casinos. We lived high until the money started to dwindle, then we found a new location and settled into a normal life there so we wouldn't call attention to ourselves. We're getting older and thought we would like to stay here for the rest of our lives, but we were getting low on money. Then, one day while Wilma was feeding Gene her usual gingerbread and coffee, he told her he was dying."

Marge closed her eyes and fought a wave of pain. Gene had confided in the Watsons—people he thought he could trust—and that had gotten him killed. Why couldn't he have confided in his wife?

Willy was still talking. "Wilma decided it was too good an opportunity to miss. She insisted we run the scam one more time, get Gene's money, and find someplace else to live out our lives. It would be safer than usual because Gene would probably die before he realized the money was gone.

"I did think about you, Margy. You were too good a friend, the closest to a daughter we would ever have. I didn't intend to leave you broke. I naturally assumed you had life insurance on Gene and would be okay after he died.

"So, we did it. We convinced Gene that I had an inside track on this investment, that he would be able to provide a comfortable life for you after he died if he moved all his money into it. He cashed out the two funds and endorsed the checks over to us. I suppose we assumed Gene had so much on his mind and trusted us enough that he wouldn't check on the investment, and after he died we would be in the clear. Anyway, we delayed making our preparations. Gene figured things out awfully fast. He came over a few days before he died to tell us he knew everything; but because we had been such good friends he'd keep quiet if we returned the money and never pulled a stunt like that again." Willy ducked his head. "He looked crushed."

"Willy, you're talking foolish. I don't know where you get such ideas. You'd better stop, before you end up in an asylum," Wilma interrupted. Her voice was beginning to sound shrill, the look in her eyes betraying her fear.

Willy looked at her, his eyes vacant. "I told Gene we would return the money. I really wanted to do it, but I knew Wilma wouldn't let me. Instead, she talked me into getting more money by running the scam on Frank, then we'd leave town. By the time we got Frank's money, Gene was about to come back to get his, so we went to the airport and spent the night in a hotel before our early morning flight.

"Before leaving the hotel room in the morning, we saw it on the news. I thought Gene had gone to our house and found it deserted. He would have been desperate. I figured he killed himself for the insurance, to make sure you had money to live on after he was gone. Wilma was happy. She said we didn't have to leave after all. No one would ever connect us with it.

"I wouldn't have come back, but I wanted to make sure you were all right. By the time we got to the house, things had settled down at your place. I guess everyone was in your house, so no one noticed us return to ours."

Marge tried to remember the chaos of that morning. No, she hadn't seen the Watsons among the neighbors that gathered when the police cars arrived. She had been too overcome with Gene's death to notice at the time. It was the next afternoon when Wilma came over with the first of many casseroles.

Marge swallowed hard. It was difficult to speak, but she had to know everything. "So, with Gene dead you didn't need to leave after all. What about Frank?"

"With Gene dead and my investment knowledge, we had enough money to spend the rest of our lives right here in Bellevue, so we made the investment for Frank and thought that was the end of it."

"Which it would have been if we hadn't traced both investments to the same company."

"Stupid idiot," Wilma said. "Using the same company." She seemed to collect herself. "If I had any part of this, I wouldn't have done anything so stupid," she quickly added.

"But it didn't matter when we thought we were leaving town. By the time anyone figured out what had happened we should have been long gone."

"You must have picked up Gene's keys when you were in and out of my house all the time."

"You gave them to us, so we could come and go when you were so helpless, don't you remember?" Wilma's grin was frightening in its unexpected sweetness. Marge couldn't decide whether she really had given them the keys or whether Wilma was trying to torment her. "Since we were going on vacation and you were out, Willy threw them into your yard. I don't know why the idiot didn't just slip them into your mailbox, but that's Willy for you." The look Wilma leveled at him could have melted steel. There was no trace of the loving wife she had appeared to be for the past six years.

Marge tried to get more information out of them, but

Willy seemed to have drifted somewhere far away and Wilma continued to glare, first at Willy and then at Marge. A few minutes later, Detective Peterson opened the door and motioned Marge out.

"I told you I got the results of their fingerprint check," the detective told her when they were seated in his office. "They are wanted in Florida, Arizona, New Mexico, and California for fraud. Not for murder, though."

"You were listening?" Marge asked.

"Yes. Actually, we got it on tape."

"Can you use it in court?"

He shrugged. "I think Willy has broken. It's only a matter of time until he cops to the murder, too, unless your husband really did kill himself. It looks like Wilma was the instigator of their life of crime. True to form, every time they ran their swindle it was a little bolder, the take a little larger. Still, it cost a lot to create new identities and move around like that. Especially since they paid cash for their houses and abandoned them when they left. Your money would have set them up nicely, especially if they didn't have to move.

"By the way, Willy really was a successful broker, the star of his firm many years ago, until shortly after his marriage, when he got caught mishandling customers' money. In his suitcase he had a few certificates for outstanding customer service—from his early years at the firm. Some had the dates forged to make them seem to cover a longer period of time. That probably helped people like your husband trust his judgment more than they otherwise would have."

"What about the money?" Marge asked. "When can I get it back?"

"You'll be lucky if you do. Money swindled like this usually disappears. It could even be in one of those infamous

Swiss or Cayman Island bank accounts, to which we don't have access. Although this is beyond my expertise and out of my hands, given the Watsons' past, if any money is recovered, I expect it will have many claimants. There is a chance you'll get *something* eventually—but nothing like what you lost."

"But, they must have stolen over a million dollars," Marge exclaimed. "They can't have spent it all. They lived quite simply."

"You forget about those trips they took," Detective Peterson said, "and their need to abandon their homes every time they moved. If they needed your husband's money in order to finish their lives in comfort, they can't have had much put away. Perhaps the prospect of poverty in their old age was enough to push them over the edge and make them kill your husband."

"I don't think they killed Gene," she said.

The detective gave her one of his searching looks. "So, you think he killed himself?"

"No. I think something more is going on. Willy talked about the money from our savings. He never mentioned the business check. Remember, I said I had something else to tell you? It looks like Bruce Wilcox, Gene's business partner, might have lied about buying Gene out. The records show a third partner was added to the firm."

"Didn't you say Wilcox showed you a receipt for the check? And didn't he say he needed a new partner to take over your husband's share?"

"Yes, I saw the receipt; but I was in a state of shock when I did. Plus I wouldn't know if something was funny about it. Did you look at it?"

"Yes, I did. It was a properly executed receipt."

Marge felt a wave of weakness at his dismissal of the

receipt. "Also, Gene's name was still listed as a partner in the firm when the new one was added. His name was never removed."

Detective Peterson sighed. "Perhaps an oversight?"

"The endorsed check. Did you look at that?" Marge asked. She heard her voice come out high, felt herself beginning to lose control. The look the detective gave her was long and appraising. When he spoke, his voice was dismissive.

"Let me summarize, Mrs. Christensen. First, you said the Watsons couldn't be guilty of anything, then you said they were guilty of fraud and murder. Now that we have them under arrest, you have decided they are innocent of murder. Instead, it was Bruce Wilcox who killed your husband."

Marge sighed. "I don't know that Bruce killed Gene. I can't figure out why he would." At the detective's raised eyebrows, Marge scowled in thought and added, "I know the buyout was a lot of money, but Bruce had another partner coming in who would put the same amount back into the business."

"So, what are you saying?" Detective Peterson asked.

"Just that we're not finished," she said. "We don't know everything yet."

The detective gave Marge another long appraising look, making her squirm. He sighed deeply. "Mrs. Christensen, we have the people who stole your money. Either they killed your husband or he committed suicide. You go home and sleep on it. I think you'll see things more clearly in the morning. And, by then, we may have a confession from Willy for the whole thing."

CHAPTER 13

MARGE WENT HOME, but not to sleep. After preparing and nibbling at dinner, she sat in the rocking chair and rocked hard as her mind grappled with what was bothering her. She didn't know what made her so sure, but she was certain neither Willy nor Wilma killed Gene. But, if they hadn't, who then? Bruce? How was she going to find out? And how was she going to prove it to Detective Peterson?

Two checks, Willy had said. They only got the two checks. So, the business check was still missing. Could Frank have talked Gene out of the business money? And made his investment with it in order to hide from Lori the money he spent on his mistress? But, why would Gene have entrusted Frank with money to invest? Frank had no investment experience. It was enough of a stretch that Gene had given money to Willy. At least Willy knew investments, though he hadn't made it public knowledge. No matter how Marge looked at it, the only one left was Bruce.

Gene had signed a receipt for Bruce's check for his half of the business. He must have received the check otherwise he wouldn't have signed the receipt. But he didn't deposit it in his account. Did he endorse it directly over to someone else? Did he cash it somewhere else? In either case, Bruce's bank should have a copy of the cancelled check. However, the police weren't going to look at it and there was no way the bank was going to give her access.

Marge crawled into bed; but sleep wouldn't come. At eleven o'clock she got up, thinking about the receipt Bruce had shown her. She was sure it was Gene's signature. She wished she had looked at it closer. That's where the trail started. She had to get another look at the receipt. She also wanted to see if there was anything else Bruce was hiding.

Would Bruce let her see it again? Probably not, if he had anything to hide and knew she was getting suspicious. Bruce would keep those files safely locked in his office and obstruct any effort Marge made to find out what they contained.

Hardly aware of what she was doing, Marge dressed, found an old office key she had nearly thrown away, one Bruce and Gene had apparently forgotten about. She quietly slipped into the Honda and headed toward Bellevue.

To keep costs down, Bruce and Gene had rented office space in a strip mall a short distance from downtown Bellevue. Marge glanced at dark menacing doorways as she parked the Honda at the curb across the street. With no late-night establishments in the area, the mall appeared deserted; the only illumination came from widely spaced streetlights and occasional cars driving by. Shadows hovered over the parking area.

Marge took a flashlight from the glove compartment, pulled her collar up against the drizzle, and hurried across the street to the office door. The key fit and turned easily. She slipped through the door and quickly closed it behind her.

She didn't bother to stop at the receptionist's desk. If she was going to find anything, it would be in Bruce's office. She breathed a sigh of relief when she found his door open. Using light that filtered in through the front windows, she found her way into the office and made sure the window shades were closed before closing the office door behind her and flicking on the flashlight.

She remembered the drawer from which Bruce had pulled the receipt. On legs suddenly so shaky she wasn't sure they would hold her, she made her way to the file cabinet and pulled on the drawer. It was locked.

Panic filled her throat with a sour taste, making her mind go blank. A few deep breaths steadied her. Marge swung the flashlight over the desk and saw the green marble paperweight. She gasped with relief when she opened the box and found the key.

Kneeling down behind the desk and putting the flashlight on the chair, aimed at the file cabinet, Marge fit the key in the lock and opened the drawer. She pulled out a folder with Gene's name on it, then leafed through the remaining files. The new partner's file was there, one for the landlord, and folders for various office expenses. Her hand stopped. Life insurance, one folder each for Bruce, Gene, and the new partner. Of course, partners in a business would have life insurance on each other. But, if Bruce had bought Gene out, wouldn't it have been cancelled? She pulled that folder, too, picked up the flashlight, and sat in Bruce's leather chair.

She opened the insurance folder first. The policy on Gene, with Bruce as beneficiary, was for five hundred thousand dollars. Marge gasped. That was more than the partners had put into the business. She glanced at the other two policies and saw that they were the same amount. Evidently the insurance company allowed whatever the partners wanted to pay for.

The only other item in the folder was a copy of a letter from Bruce to the insurance company, informing it of Gene's death and requesting payment of the face value of the policy.

Marge stared at the letter in disbelief. Bruce hadn't cancelled the policy when he bought Gene out. He had somehow gotten a copy of the death certificate. While Marge ended up with nothing, Bruce walked away with five hundred thousand dollars. After Gene was no longer a partner. Or—was he? Gene's name was still on the partnership agreement in the public records.

The door burst open. Marge jumped, nearly falling out of the chair. She closed her eyes against the glare of light that suddenly filled the room.

"What the hell are you doing in here?" Bruce's voice demanded.

Marge opened her eyes to see Bruce in the doorway, two uniformed policemen right behind him. She sunk back down into the chair, as if trying to make herself disappear.

"I . . . I . . ." Her voice was a low squeak.

Bruce's eyes narrowed when he saw the folder in her hand. He reached for it, but Marge held onto it tightly.

"Give me that. That is private information," he ordered.

Marge looked desperately at the police officer nearest her. "Please, call Detective Pete Peterson," she said, finding her voice. "I just found the motive for my husband's murder."

"Who might you be?" the officer asked. "And what are

you doing in Mr. Wilcox's office, in the dark, at this time of night?"

"I'm trying to find out why he killed my husband," Marge said. "If you'll call Detective Peterson I'm sure we can straighten this out."

"Do you know this woman?" the officer asked Bruce.

"Yes, she is the wife of my former partner, who committed suicide six weeks ago. She's been trying to find a nonexistent murderer ever since."

Marge stared at Bruce, stung. He made it sound like she had been harassing him for six weeks, when she had only spoken to him once last week. If she needed any convincing that he killed Gene, his efforts to make her look foolish achieved it nicely.

"Please," she begged, turning to the officer again. "If Bruce is innocent, it will do no harm to call the detective."

"Have you found something that incriminates Mr. Wilcox? Something that would justify your breaking and entering?"

"This life insurance policy," she said. "It gives him a motive."

Bruce snorted. "You're delusional, Marge. Of course I had life insurance on Gene. Since I kept up payments, it was still in effect. There is nothing illegal about that. Perhaps you are upset because you think I should have shared it with you, considering your loss of the rest of your savings—but your loss wasn't my fault."

"Do you want us to arrest her, Mr. Wilcox?"

Bruce tugged at the file folders. "No," he said. "She is still distraught over her husband's death."

Marge pulled back on the folders, catching Bruce by surprise. Just as quickly, she released them. They fell to the floor. When they both bent down to pick up the folders, Marge let Bruce grab the insurance folder while she flipped open the other one. She only had time for a quick look at the receipt for the buyout before Bruce grabbed that folder, too, but since she knew what she was looking for that moment was enough.

When they stood, Bruce's eyes were narrowed. "How did you get in here, Marge?" he asked.

"I jimmied the lock," she said, hoping the lie wasn't as transparent as she felt.

"I don't think so. I think you have a key Gene left around." He held out his hand. "Let's have it." His eyes moved to the open marble box. "And the key to the file cabinet, too."

After a moment's hesitation, Marge handed him the keys.

He turned to the police, motioning for them to take her. "Please go home and forget about this nonsense, before I regret I didn't have you arrested." He reached out his hand as if to put it on her shoulder, but Marge jerked away and he dropped it.

Taking a last look at the files that might still contain something incriminating, Marge slouched to the door. She turned back. "So, Gene told you he was going to die and asked you to buy him out." She stated it as a fact.

"Yes . . ." He stopped and Marge thought she saw a momentary crack in his confidence. Bruce recovered quickly. "No. I told you why he said he wanted out."

Marge stared at him. She didn't believe him. Gene had told two people he was dying, and both had betrayed him.

At a slight pressure from the policeman's hand she continued out of the office and crawled into the Honda. Before closing the car door, she looked up at the policeman.

"How did you know I was in there?" she asked.

The officer grinned. "Silent alarm. Rang at the station and Mr. Wilcox's home at the same time."

Marge shook her head. She'd make a pretty dumb burglar. She drove home with the police cruiser following her all the way.

The rest of the night Marge tossed and turned. Gene's presence seemed to permeate the bedroom, as if wanting something from her. "What more can I do?" she cried. "What did you do with the check Bruce gave you?" The presence lingered, but no answer came.

At eight-thirty the next morning, as she was drinking her second cup of coffee, the phone rang.

"Mrs. Christensen, what do you think you are doing skulking around someone else's property in the middle of the night?"

"Detective Peterson, I was about to call you."

"Call me Pete," rolled off his tongue. "I'm sure you were. Now, can you explain your actions?"

"You wouldn't do anything, and I knew something was wrong. I found a life insurance policy for five hundred thousand dollars that Bruce carried on Gene as a partner. He cashed in that policy, even though Gene was no longer a partner."

"There is nothing criminal about that," the detective said. "As long as the premiums were paid, the policy would stay in effect."

"But it gives him a motive. And I saw the receipt again. It is dated the day Gene died. If Gene got the check that day, he should have had it on him. We would have found it.

But, Bruce said Gene left the partnership a month before that, and the new partner was registered two weeks after Gene left."

"So, it took some time for Wilcox to get the money together. And your husband gave the check to the Watsons. I don't see the problem."

"The day before Gene died he had a phone conversation from the church where he was doing some volunteer work. Someone overheard Gene's side of the conversation. He said Gene was upset, and said he overheard Gene tell the person on the other end he'd be by to pick up something the next day and it better be ready or Gene would be going to the police. I believe he was talking with Bruce, who told him he could come by and pick up his check."

"That's pretty thin for evidence," the detective said, but his voice was thoughtful.

Marge pressed on, almost crying with frustration. "The new partner had to buy in, and that money should have been used to pay Gene for his share. Why the two-week delay? The life insurance gives Bruce a motive to kill Gene. Besides, what could Gene have done with the check in such a short time? Willy says they got two checks endorsed over to them from Gene. We know that's true because Gene just got the check from Bruce the day he died. But, Gene didn't have a chance to deposit the check and it wasn't on him when he died. Isn't there any way you can get a look at Bruce's account to see what happened to it?"

The detective sighed. "If Mr. Wilcox will allow us access to his account and the check was properly endorsed by your husband, will that satisfy you? Will you back off and accept things the way they are?"

Marge had no choice but to agree. It was the only way to get the detective to continue investigating. But, she was quite sure Bruce wouldn't allow the police to look at his bank account.

Robert called a few minutes later.

"Mother? What are you doing? First Kate tells me you tackled the Watsons at the airport while they were trying to escape, then Bruce calls and tells me I'd better keep you away from him."

Marge sighed. Bruce sized up people well enough to know which of her children to call to warn her off.

"I'm trying to find out who killed your father, and it looks like it might have been Bruce. Though it was the Watsons who stole our savings."

The line was silent for a moment. "I thought you were going to turn this over to the police. You've got no business snooping around someone else's property at night," Robert said. "I don't want you to end up in jail for breaking and entering."

"I didn't break anything. I had a key. And, I will go to jail if that's what it takes to find the person who killed your father."

"Mother, I hardly know you when you're like this," Robert said, fear in his voice.

"Robert, I think you hardly know me at all," she replied. "I've been hiding my self under a bushel basket since before you were born."

Marge stared at the phone after hanging it up, the truth of her words washing over her. Yes, she had been hiding. Gene never asked her to do it. She did what she thought was best for Gene and the family and ignored her own needs. Ultimately, she resented what she had become. She was so unhappy she nearly had an affair. She had no one to blame but herself.

No wonder Caroline disliked her.

The phone rang. Marge was surprised to hear from Detective Peterson so soon. "Mr. Wilcox won't allow us to look into his bank records and the judge says we don't have enough to get a court order."

"Well, that's a no-brainer. He has something to hide. What if we can prove who Gene talked with the day before he died?"

"If we find out it was Wilcox, we can try again with the judge."

Marge told him where the church phone was.

"I'll get the number and the record of calls made from it that day. You sit tight."

Marge nearly laughed. He sounded as fearful as Robert that she would get into more trouble.

She was worried, though. Since Bruce knew he was under suspicion, what would he do? Would he try to run away, like the Watsons? She didn't imagine the police had enough evidence to put him under surveillance.

How could she leave the house? Detective Peterson expected her to wait for his call. She looked across the street. Lori hadn't gone to work. Marge ran over and banged on the door.

"You have a cell phone, don't you?" she asked.

"Yes. Why?"

"Can I borrow it? I need to be somewhere, but Detective Peterson may want to get in touch with me."

Lori gave her a worried look. "Are you getting into trouble again?" she asked.

Marge grinned, feeling a rush of adrenaline. "Maybe.

But I think all I have to do is watch a door. If anything happens, I can phone the police and they will take over."

"Are you sure? Maybe I should come along, just in case."

"I can't promise I won't end up doing something illegal. Like I did last night," Marge said.

"I'm definitely coming. I want to hear what you did last night." Lori ran in to get the cell phone before joining Marge in the Honda. On the way to Bruce's office, Lori called and left the number where Detective Peterson could reach Marge. Then Marge told Lori about Willy's confession and about breaking into Bruce Wilcox's office.

They found a parking spot down the block and across the street from Bruce's office. Bruce's car was parked in front of the office. Marge reached to the backseat for the floppy hat she kept handy for Seattle's infrequent sunshine, which played havoc with her freckles. Adding sunglasses, she got out of the car and approached the building. She slid around to Bruce's office window. Peering in, she saw him moving around, filling a box with papers. Satisfied that he was planning to run but wasn't gone yet, Marge returned to the car.

Half an hour later Lori went out and purchased two cups of Starbuck's coffee. "Good thing they have one of those espresso stands on every corner these days," she said with a grin.

Another thirty minutes went by before Bruce started loading the trunk of his car. Marge took the phone and called the police station.

"I'm sorry, Detective Peterson is unavailable. May I take a message?"

"You need to get in touch with him right away," Marge said. "The man who killed my husband is cleaning out his office and getting ready to leave town."

Bruce emerged from the door of the office with a man Marge presumed to be his new partner following. The man did not look happy. Bruce ignored him, got into his BMW, and drove out of the lot.

"Oh, boy," Marge said as she started the Honda and pulled out two cars behind him. "I hoped the police would get here in time to do any tailing."

Marge tried to keep three cars between them as Bruce made his way out of the downtown area. It was easy on the busy streets but became difficult when he turned onto the side streets.

"It looks like he's going home first," Marge said. "Good, that gives us a little more time." She slowed down to increase the distance between the cars.

The cell phone finally rang after they had parked two blocks down from Bruce's house. "What do you think you're doing?" Detective Peterson asked when Lori handed Marge the phone.

"I'm keeping an eye on our prime suspect, who just cleaned out his office and seems to be doing the same thing at home," she said, trying to sound like the detectives she saw on TV.

"It seems you're having fun," Detective Peterson said, his voice heavy with disapproval.

Marge laughed, then sobered. "I won't be if we don't catch Bruce. Were you able to trace a phone number to him?"

"Yes, and along with your report that he cleaned out his office it was enough to get a look at his bank accounts. There was no check written to your husband, but there is a gap in the check numbers around the date it would have been written. Give me Bruce's address and I'll get you some backup."

Marge was only too happy to give him the information and hang up so he could get moving.

At that moment Bruce exited his house with a suitcase in hand and climbed into the driver's seat of his car. Marge didn't think she was up to a high-speed chase if he headed for the highway, which she was sure he would. She pulled away from the curb and floored the gas pedal to reach Bruce's driveway before he could get the car out. She pulled the steering wheel hard to the right, entering the driveway with a screech of tires. Lori clutched the dashboard and let out a squeal. Marge yanked hard to the left before braking, leaving the Honda on a slant that blocked the entire entrance to the driveway.

"What the hell do you think you're doing?" Bruce yelled, jumping out of the BMW. "Get out of my yard."

"Not on your life," Marge said, her voice all sweetness. "You'd best just relax and wait for the police to get here."

"You're crazy. The police have nothing on me. I'm going to call them right now and have you arrested for trespassing."

Marge caught her breath as Bruce headed for the house. "Do you suppose he has a gun in there?" she asked Lori.

"Or a back way to escape?" Lori added.

"You stay here, I'll go around back," Marge said as she started to get out of the Honda.

Lori grabbed her arm. "And do what? If he has a gun you could get killed. Even if he doesn't, he's stronger than you and could hurt you."

Marge was going to argue, but a police car swung up to the curb. "Where's the suspect?" asked one of the officers.

"He ran into the house when we blocked his driveway," Marge yelled back from inside her car.

One officer headed for the house and the other ran out back. Marge was going to follow one of them, but Lori held onto her arm. They heard a shout from the policeman in the backyard and the other one raced to join him.

Bruce came flying around the other side of the house and headed straight for the Honda.

"Out of the car," he ordered, grabbing Marge through the open car door while brandishing a golf club.

"Okay, okay," she said, swinging her legs out from under the steering wheel. But instead of standing, she quickly flexed her left knee and kicked out hard. Her aim was true. Bruce yelped, dropped the golf club, and fell to the ground grabbing his crotch as the two policemen appeared in front of the house and Detective Peterson's car pulled up behind the Honda.

"Good shot," Lori exclaimed, her face ashen despite the wide grin.

"I'll say," Detective Peterson boomed as the two officers scooped Bruce up and escorted him to the squad car. "Where did you learn that little trick?"

Marge shrugged. "It just sort of came to me," she said, wondering at it herself.

She looked at Bruce, handcuffed and being placed in the back of the police car.

"I wonder how he did it," she said.

"That we have to find out," said the detective. "It had to have been done at his office, when your husband went there to pick up the check. Maybe Wilcox gave something to Gene to put him to sleep. Something that would be covered up by the carbon monoxide. I think we'll ask Mr. Wilcox if he has any ideas about what that might have been." He turned, his steel-gray eyes squinted. "Marge Christensen, are you finally satisfied? Please tell me you are satisfied that your husband's murderer has been found."

Marge smiled faintly, suddenly so weak she thought she might melt onto the floor of the Honda. "Yes, Detective Peterson," she managed to say, "if you can make the case against Bruce stick, it is over."

"Call me Pete," he said over his shoulder as he returned to his car. "I'll follow you ladies home to make sure you get there without further problems."

Lori walked around the car and pushed Marge into the passenger seat. "You're in no shape to drive . . . again," she said. "I hope the car is," she added with a giggle.

When Marge and Lori returned to Marge's house—with a police backup—Frank was watching from his doorway.

"Shouldn't you go home to him or something?" Marge asked.

"He can wait," Lori said, steel in her voice. Marge knew that whatever happened to their marriage, Lori was going to be all right.

CHAPTER 14

IT WAS OVER. Kate whooped with joy when Marge told her. Robert audibly sighed with relief. They both said they were on their way over and that Marge was not to prepare anything. Beer and pizza would do for a celebration.

Which was good. Marge didn't think she could find two consecutive thoughts in her head to decide on any sort of meal.

Marge insisted Detective Peterson join them after he finished interrogating Bruce. She wanted to know every detail, so she could put it all behind her.

She called Lori and Frank, since they were involved. And Melissa, too, since she was a new confidante and deserved to be in on the story. And, finally, after some hesitating, she phoned Charles. She tried to find a number for Larry, but evidently he still didn't have a phone. She'd drive out to give him the news as soon as possible.

For some reason, Marge thought of asking David to come over, but she pushed the idea aside. It was inappropriate. He didn't know Gene and she couldn't think of any plausible explanation for having him there.

Tonight would be the memorial service they couldn't have while the shadow hung over Gene's name.

Once everyone but Detective Peterson had gathered, Lori and Marge recounted the happenings of the last two days. Robert's brown eyes were round as a small boy's when being told a tall tale. "How could you act so, so . . ." He couldn't find the words to express his anguish.

Melissa was impressed. "I guess you proved you can handle life on your own," she said.

Kate, for a change, was speechless, her green eyes staring at Marge in wonderment and pride.

Caroline was quiet, which made Marge nervous. But then, the perfect lines of her face broke into a wide grin. "Way to go, Marge." she said. "Who'd of thunk it?"

Charles moved closer to Marge, his arm rising to drape over her shoulders, as if claiming her for his own. Marge deftly sidestepped. Turning, to be sure no one else could hear her, she said softly but firmly, "Not anymore, Charles."

He opened his mouth, as if to argue. She leveled a steady gaze at him and he closed it again. Something clicked shut in his eyes, and she knew he understood.

Detective Peterson arrived at eight o'clock, looking more tired than Marge had ever seen him.

"Are you off duty, Detective Peterson? Can I offer you a beer? Or a drink, if you prefer?" Marge asked.

"Call me Pete, *please*. Yes, I'm finished—unless you've come up with something more to keep me from getting bored," he said. "And, if you have scotch, I'll take it on the rocks."

He waited until Marge brought his drink before telling everyone what happened at the station.

"The Watsons were made of sterner stuff than your Bruce Wilcox. He fell apart as soon as we got him into the interrogation room.

"You were right, Mrs. Christensen. Wilcox stalled paying your husband until your husband threatened him with legal action. He did it because he didn't have the money. With child support, two house payments, gambling, and girls, he was in debt up to his eyeballs. When Gene told him about his illness . . ."

Marge felt the pain again that Gene hadn't told her. Though it wouldn't have made any difference in the outcome, she reminded herself.

". . . he saw a way to solve his problems by keeping the business money and collecting on your husband's life insurance. So, when Gene arrived to pick up his check, Bruce was waiting with a brandy to celebrate. Only Mr. Christensen's brandy was laced with enough of the painkiller Percodan to put him to sleep within a few minutes.

"As lightweight as Gene had become with his illness, it was easy for Wilcox to put him in his BMW, drive him home, push him into the driver's seat, crack the window and leave the motor running, and finally hit the button to close the garage door and slip out before it closed. Wilcox walked a couple of miles before catching a bus downtown and taking a cab back to the office to retrieve his car."

"Wouldn't the brandy have tasted funny?" Charles asked, swirling the amber liquid in his own glass.

"Gene probably wouldn't know the difference," Marge said. "He never drank brandy; only beer and scotch."

Kate walked over, tears making her green eyes sparkle. She threw her arms around Marge. "Thank you, Mom.

Thank you so much for hanging in there and proving Daddy didn't kill himself. I tried to convince myself it didn't really matter how he died, but it did. It did."

"Oh, Willy Watson asked me to thank you," Detective Peterson said. "He'll take his lumps for stealing the money, though he won't produce any of it to pay you back. He's still taking care of his 'baby' first. But, at least he doesn't have to feel responsible for your husband's death on top of it.

"And, you might be interested to know that he is going to plead guilty to the fraud on his own. He won't implicate Wilma. She may get out of this altogether, and she has access to the money."

"She won't be able to get to it, will she?" Robert asked. "Won't you be watching out for that?"

"I have a feeling it is in a safe account overseas, Switzerland or some place like that. If Willy pleads guilty and refuses to implicate Wilma, the DA may decide not to pursue the case against Wilma at all. She could leave the country without a hitch and live happily ever after."

"What about the insurance money Bruce collected?" Robert asked. "Can Mother get any of that?"

"I don't see how she could. The insurance company will sue for repayment because it doesn't pay a beneficiary who commits murder to get the money. But it has no obligation to pay anyone other than the beneficiary."

Robert turned to Marge. "What will you do, Mother? The money from the house and BMW won't last forever."

Marge shrugged. Her wine seemed to fill her with confidence. "I'll think of something," she said. After all, she thought, if she could attack a man in an airport, break into an office in the middle of the night, and kick an attacker where it did the most good, she could probably figure out a way to find the lost money and to manage her future. She knew she wasn't going to give up on finding the money quite yet.

Melissa grinned and winked, as if reading Marge's thoughts.

After everyone left, Marge wandered around the house. It seemed larger and emptier than it ever had. It took her awhile to realize it was because Gene no longer lurked around the corners or hovered, waiting for her to clear his name. She knew she would never hear him talk to her again. The loss hit Marge with an impact that stopped her pacing, the pain was as complete and severe as it had been at any-time since Gene's death. She took a deep breath and walked into the kitchen.

Taking out a pad of paper and a pencil, she went through the house once more, listing the furniture she would need to get rid of before settlement time on the house and writing down the more immediate tasks.

Tomorrow she would call the temporary agency to let them know she was ready for another assignment.

She would begin a serious search for her next home.

She would phone David Walters to give him the second set of keys to the BMW. The idea gave her such a warm glow, she quickly went on to other chores.

Excitement welled within her. Gene's name had been cleared, so he could rest in peace. She had nothing to worry about except building her own future and finding her money.

And she would learn to find happiness in the only source that she would never lose: herself.

Don't miss Marge Christensen's next mystery . . .

Why Did You
DIE IN THE PARK?

Turn the page for a special preview . . .

Why Did You Die in the Park?

A year has passed since Marge solved the mystery of her husband, Gene's, untimely death. She is finally settled into a new apartment and comfortable with her life. It is a warm April day and she decides to take a walk in nearby Kelsey Creek Park.

As Marge steps down the slight slope, planting her feet carefully with each step so that she doesn't slip on the soggy leaves that accumulated last autumn, her eye catches a glimpse of light blue on the ground ahead. Curious as to what spring flower has emerged, she walks toward the unexpected color.

Not wanting to get her walking boots too muddied, she peers over some bushes and notices a mound of damp brown earth and freshly exposed roots and broken branches. Hmmm. The patch of blue looks like a denim shirt. She frowns and walks closer. The second she sees a dirt-encrusted hand sticking out of the ground nearby, she realizes it *is* a denim shirt—and a flashback of Gene's lifeless body slumped in the front seat of his BMW engulfs her.

Something is wrong. She grasps for the trunk of a tree to steady herself. She is frozen to the spot where she stands.

Her throat is tight and she wills her eyes to open. To look again.

Why did she veer off the hiking trail at this particular spot? What twist of fate dictated that she should be the one to find the body?

Marge Christensen has no intention of getting involved with another murder . . . until Frank, her best friend Lori's husband, is accused of the crime. And then both Lori and Frank accuse Marge of drawing police attention to Frank, where it is likely to stay unless someone can convince the police to turn in another direction.

That someone is going to have to be Marge.

Detective Pete Peterson is as set against Marge involving herself with this case as he was with her husband's death last year. But he also seems determined to accept everything that points to Frank's guilt, while downplaying anything that might prove Frank innocent.

Marge is beginning to think this particular detective has a blind spot where murder is concerned. And, even though the unfolding circumstances tend to support Detective Peterson's belief, Marge hangs onto her presumption of Frank's innocence in order to dig deeper and find the real suspect.

ABOUT THE AUTHOR

⌇

WHEN PATRICIA K. BATTA'S fourth grade teacher instructed the class to write a story, she did. And, Patricia was so thrilled with the process of creating a different world on paper, she wrote another one, and another one, and another one . . .

Batta has a bachelor's degree from the University of Puerto Rico and a master's degree in teaching from Oberlin College. After teaching elementary school in Ohio and Pennsylvania, she moved to Seattle, Washington, where she resided for twenty-one years. After her husband's death, Batta returned to her hometown of Traverse City, Michigan.

Over the years Batta wrote sporadically and, by the time she retired, two mysteries were written and a third begun. *What Did You Do Before Dying?* is the first in a series of Marge Christensen mysteries.

Watch for the sequel in 2009.